Joe stopped as he came into the waiting room and saw Rachael.

'Uh…hi.' Then he looked at the person by her side. Rachael dropped her arm from around Declan's waist and clenched her hands tightly in an effort to control the feeling of dread which swamped her.

Rachael watched as Joe looked the boy up and down before slowly shaking his head. 'Er…Joe.' She cleared her throat and forced the words out. 'I'd like you to meet Declan. My son.'

'Joe?' Declan asked, and Rachael turned to look up at him. She nodded. '*The* Joe?'

Rachael nodded again.

'My *dad*—Joe?'

Rachael glanced at her son, then Joe. 'Yes.'

Lucy Clark began writing romance in her early teens and immediately knew she'd found her 'calling' in life. After working as a secretary in a busy teaching hospital, she turned her hand to writing medical romance. She currently lives in South Australia with her husband and two children. Lucy largely credits her writing success to the support of her husband, family and friends.

Recent titles by the same author:

DR CUSACK'S SECRET SON

BY
LUCY CLARK

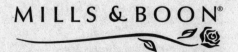

MILLS & BOON®

To my sister Claire,
Here is your Joseph. I hope you love him as much as I do.
1 John 1:9

First published in Great Britain 2005
Harlequin Mills & Boon Limited,
Eton House, 18-24 Paradise Road, Richmond, Surrey TW9 1SR

© Lucy Clark 2005

ISBN 0 263 84299 1

Set in Times Roman 10¼ on 11½ pt.
03-0405-51441

Printed and bound in Spain
by Litografía Rosés, S.A., Barcelona

CHAPTER ONE

'YOU'RE late—*again*!'

Joe grinned at his practice manager. 'Good morning, Helen.' He leaned over the receptionist's counter and gave her a kiss on the cheek. 'What's the good in owning a practice if I can't set my own hours?'

Helen pretended to consider this. 'Hmm, is it because you have patients waiting for you?'

Joe turned and scanned the empty waiting room. 'Are they hiding?'

'No. Mrs Taub called to say she was running late and I bet you've forgotten the other reason I asked you to be early today.'

Joe frowned, thinking hard. 'You're right. I've forgotten.'

'Honestly, Joe. You've a brain like a sieve some days.'

'I'm going to take that as a compliment.' He picked up his patient files and started up the corridor. Helen stopped him.

'The new locum starts today.'

'We have a new locum?'

'Joseph,' she said in that reprimanding voice of hers which never failed to bring a smile to his face. 'You knew Alison was going on maternity leave. Don't tell me you didn't realise the doctor who's worked here for the past two years was pregnant?'

'No.' He headed into his consulting room, Helen hard on his heels. 'Hey, that means I missed her going-away party. Oops.'

'You were on set. It's all right. Alison understands but she's expecting you to visit her once she's had the baby.'

Joe shuddered. 'Do I have to? I'll send a gift but you know how babies make me feel.'

'Just because you don't want to have any children, Joe Silvermark, that's no reason not to be nice to those who do.'

Joe was instantly contrite, remembering Helen had no children of her own…which was where he'd come in. 'You're right. I apologise. When the baby's born, I will visit her. Put it in my diary and bug me until I do it.'

Helen grinned. 'Already done.'

'Good. So, I have a new locum to break in, eh? Male or female?'

'Female.'

'Is she good-looking?'

'She wears a wedding ring so it looks as though you're out of luck there but, yes, she's attractive. She also has brilliant credentials and came highly recommended from a colleague of mine. We were lucky to get her at the last minute, especially as the previous locum I had lined up pulled out without warning.'

'She was probably pregnant as well,' Joe muttered. 'Call the water board and make sure there's nothing in the water,' he joked.

'See, now, I thought she might have pulled out because she'd heard you're hardly here to do any work and would be leaving it all up to her.'

He shrugged. 'So? I own the practice, which means I can employ people to do the work for me. That leaves me free to pursue my own interests in the movie-making business.'

Helen shook her head. 'Whatever am I going to do with you, Dr Hollywood?'

'Nothing.' He grinned again. 'Where's the new recruit?'

'Either in her consulting room or the kitchen.' The bell over the front door jingled. 'Ah, there's my cue. You only have four patients this morning and then you can get back on set.'

'Right.' Both of them walked out of his consulting room—

Helen towards the reception area and Joe to the back of the old converted house he'd bought almost five years ago. He checked the other consulting room but found it empty. He breathed in deeply. 'Ah, must be coffee time.' He headed to the kitchen and stopped in the doorway when he saw a woman dressed in a navy skirt and light blue shirt with one long, dark braid hanging down her back standing at the sink, her back to him.

Joe felt an immediate tightening in his gut. It always happened when he saw a woman with hair that colour. Black, as black as the darkest night. Not many women naturally had hair that was jet black but this one did and she instantly reminded him of Rachael—the woman who'd plagued his subconscious for the past fifteen years.

Joe let out a slow breath, waiting for the tightening to disappear, but this time it didn't. He glanced at the woman's legs and shook his head. Her legs were incredible. Rachael's legs had been equally as gorgeous and the sensitive depths of her blue eyes had always been able to bring a response from him. Too bad this woman was married because she appeared to be just his type.

Joe shrugged and pushed all thoughts of Rachael back into the box where they belonged. He cleared his throat and his new colleague turned.

It was simultaneous.

The colour drained out of both their faces and they each clutched at something for support—Joe the doorframe, Rachael the sink.

Rachael's knees started to buckle and she found it hard to breathe, to concentrate, to do anything. The cup she'd been holding slipped from her hands and shattered at her feet. Thankfully, she hadn't yet filled the cup with anything but her one sugar.

She opened her mouth to speak but found it impossible to form any words. Her heart was pounding fiercely against her ribs, her head was getting lighter by the second due to lack of oxygen, and she felt the dizziness start to claim her.

Her knees gave way and she started to slide down the cupboards. 'No.' She shook her head and finally managed to tear her gaze away from him, her eyes screwed tight. 'No.' She hugged her knees to her chest, trying desperately to get control of her emotions.

This wasn't happening. This wasn't possible. How could she have been so careless? Why, oh, why hadn't she done more research, asked more questions, done her homework before starting work at this particular medical practice? Why had she blindly let her friend and colleague, Lance, set this up for her?

Her next thought was, how could she get out of it? Was it possible to renege on the contract on her first day? She knew it was highly unprofessional but she honestly didn't think she'd be able to work here for the next six months, regardless of how perfect the job had seemed to her.

Feeling her breathing begin to calm, Rachael opened her eyes and was surprised to find no one standing in the doorway. Had she imagined it? She glanced across at the shattered cup beside her. Had she hallucinated? Had she somehow conjured up the image of the man who'd shredded her soul fifteen years ago? The man she'd thought about every day since?

Slowly rising to her feet, Rachael forced herself to concentrate. She found a dustpan and brush and had just finished sweeping the mess up when Helen came into the room.

'Is everything all right?'

Rachael turned to look at her, hoping she was able to keep the look of total panic from her face. 'I broke a cup. Sorry. I'll replace it.'

'Who cares about the cup? You look as though you've seen a ghost...' Helen paused. 'And so does Joe.'

Rachael closed her eyes. 'So it was him.' The words were barely a whisper.

'You two know each other?' Helen's tone was incredulous.

Rachael looked at the other woman. 'You could say that.' Anger…anger she'd thought she'd dealt with years ago began to surface. 'He broke my heart when I was eighteen.'

It was Helen's turn to pale. 'You're *that* Rachael?'

'You know about me?' Now it was Rachael's turn to be surprised.

'I've known Joe since he was a boy and the deal back then was that we didn't keep secrets. He told me about you when he finally returned from America.' Helen shrugged. 'Not all the details but that you'd been married and had had it annulled.'

Rachael swallowed over the hurt at hearing those words. She smoothed a hand down her skirt. 'Look, Helen, I'm sorry but I can't work here with…with…Joe.' She forced herself to say his name out loud. 'I know that means leaving the patients in the lurch and it's highly unprofessional but I just can't.'

When Helen remained silent, Rachael continued. 'I've never done anything like this in my life. I've always been the dependable one. Dependable Rachael, that's me, but right now I don't even think I can depend on myself.'

'Joe's already left.'

'He walked out?' Rachael snorted as anger began to fill her once more. 'Typical. I can see he hasn't changed much in fifteen years.'

'He'll be back in about five minutes. He just needs to get his head around this, just like you do.' Helen pulled out chairs for both of them. 'Sit down a moment.' Rachael did as she was asked. 'Look, I realise this has come as a shock for both of you but perhaps it's for the best. Perhaps this is your opportunity to work through what happened so you can both get closure.'

'I got closure, Helen, when I signed our annulment papers.'

'Really?' Helen raised her eyebrows disbelievingly. 'Then

why are you so angry now?' The question hung in the air for a second before she continued. 'Look, Rachael, you were both young and—'

'Stop. I'll stay for today and do the clinic but after that I'm not coming back.'

'You'll be breaking your contract.'

'Feel free to take me to court. I'd rather pay the penalties than stay here.'

'You hate him that much?' Helen asked softly.

Rachael closed her eyes, knowing her emotions for Joe were so jumbled she doubted she could pick just one to describe how she felt. 'It's…complicated, Helen.'

'At least give me until the end of the week to find a replacement. Joe's busy on the set at the moment and he's not scheduled to finish the movie for another two months. Either way, I desperately need someone here to pick up the slack.'

'So now you want me to stay for two months?'

'Your contract is for six months, Rachael,' she pointed out.

'How about two weeks?'

Helen looked at her and Rachael silently hoped the other woman would concede. 'Two weeks.' She nodded. 'Both you and Joe will hardly see each other if that's what you want. I'll schedule different lunchbreaks and, besides, he'll be on set for at least half of every day so he won't even be here.'

'What does that mean? On set?'

'It means,' said a deep voice from the doorway, 'that he's the medical officer at the movie production studio which is a few blocks away.'

'I call him Dr Hollywood,' Helen teased, then quickly wiped the smile off her face when they both glared at her. 'It's a theme park but they also shoot movies there,' Helen added as she stood. 'Some are quite big budget ones, not just the independent films.' She glanced from one to the other, sensing the atmosphere. 'I'll give you some privacy.'

Rachael couldn't look at him. If she did, she thought she

might crumble into an unprofessional heap again and that would never do. Joe walked over and pulled out a chair at the other end of the table.

'Are you staying?'

It was amazing. He'd known she would want to leave. She shook her head, bemused by the situation for a moment. Could they still read each other's minds? 'For two weeks until Helen can get someone else.'

'Thank you.'

'Don't patronise me, Joe.'

'I wasn't.' He raised his hands in defence, waited a beat and then said softly, 'You look good, Rach.'

She closed her eyes, desperate to control her heart rate. One nice word from him and she could feel her body turning to mush, although this time it wasn't from shock but from memories of another time when he'd spoken to her in that quiet, caring tone.

Slowly, she forced herself to breathe and opened her eyes again. 'You look good, too, Joe.' Understatement of the year! He looked...incredible. He looked better than her fifteen-year-old memory recalled. Ruggedly handsome with that rebel-without-a-cause attitude which had attracted her to him in the first place. He was also dead sexy.

Instead of the tight denim jeans and leather jacket which had been his standard wardrobe back then, he now wore a crisp cotton shirt, opened to the neck, and a pair of trousers. Still casual but more...grown up. His dark brown hair was more under control than the messy way he'd worn it back then and there was a hint of grey at his temples, which lent him a distinguished air. Joe? Distinguished? She smiled at the thought and shook her head. People didn't change *that* much.

'That's funny?'

'What?'

'That I look good.' He had that teasing tone to his voice

and she admitted to herself that she'd missed his humour. He'd always been able to make her laugh.

Her smile started to fade. 'That's not what made me smile. I guess we'd better see to our patients.' She prayed, as she pushed to her feet, that her legs would support her. Thankfully, they did but she didn't let go of the table until she was perfectly sure.

'I'll have Helen bring you in a cup of coffee once you're settled.'

'Thank you.' My, oh, my, weren't they the polite ones?

'Still milk and two sugars?'

'Uh…' Rachael faltered. He remembered how she'd taken her coffee? Was that right? Was he supposed to remember things like that after fifteen years? She cleared her throat, feeling her earlier strength leave her, and reached for the chair to steady herself. 'Uh…no. Actually, I have it black with one sugar.'

Joe clenched his jaw but nodded as she walked from the room. Black with one sugar. That was how he took his coffee and he was the one who'd forced her to try it without milk. Had she changed after that experience? He shook his head as the image of them both wearing matching hotel robes, sitting in the middle of a bed tasting each other's coffee, flooded his mind. Their two days of heaven. Two days of being shut away from the world in a small hotel room in Las Vegas. Two days of wedded bliss where Joe had thought his life had changed for ever because of the love he'd found with Rachael.

'Reality bites.' He shoved the memory away. Now that he'd recovered from the shock of seeing her, here, in the Gold Coast—at his medical practice—Joe began to realise that one memory after another would continue to intrude.

Maybe it was time. Time to face up to what had happened between them all those years ago. She'd agreed to stay for two weeks so maybe, just maybe, he might be able to get some closure. He had regrets and had always secretly hoped

for the opportunity to set the record straight, and now he had
his chance. He made a mental note to himself not to blow it,
not this time.

Joe went to the waiting room, asked Helen to take Rachael
a cup of coffee and, seeing that Mrs Taub had arrived, called
her through. He'd heard Helen telling Rachael she wouldn't
have to see him and, although he knew Rachael would prefer
to hightail it out of here as soon as possible, Joe wasn't going
to knock this opportunity back. Rachael Cusack was unfin-
ished business as far as he was concerned, and he was determined in the next two weeks to finish that business once and
for all.

Rachael looked down at her patient list. Two more to go.
Thank goodness. She sat at her desk for a moment and placed
her head in her hands, resting her elbows on the desk. She
was mentally and physically exhausted. Never had keeping up
the pretence of being OK been so hard in her life. Then again,
it wasn't every day a woman ran into the man of her dreams.

And that's exactly what Joe Silvermark had been, she told
herself sternly. Just a dream. A fantasy that had gone horribly
wrong. It had taken her a long time to come to grips with
what had happened all those years ago but finally, eventually
she'd managed to get on with her life. She'd thought she was
over Joe.

Rachael lifted her head and sighed. Who was she trying to
kid? After the first initial shock, an amazing surge of desire
had spread through her entire body like wildfire. She was not
only still attracted to the man but wanted him more than she'd
ever wanted anything in her life. After all, she remembered
exactly how Joe could make her feel.

'This isn't getting your work done,' she told herself as she
stood and glanced at the clock. Quarter to four! Declan would
be here soon. Her breath caught in her throat. *Declan!*

Rachael's knees started to shake and she quickly sat down

again. Declan. She closed her eyes, trying to control her breathing. How was she going to tell him? How was she going to tell Joe? When Declan arrived, she knew that one look at her son would tell Joe the whole story. Ah, but Joe wasn't here this afternoon. Hadn't Helen said as much?

Hoping for a reprieve, she breathed a sigh of relief. She knew she had to tell Joe the truth and she would, but she'd hoped for a little more time to come to terms with everything. Rachael bit her lip. Would Joe want to be a part of Declan's life? She'd never lied to her son, and as he'd grown older they'd openly discussed Joe. She'd always told Declan if he'd wanted to find his father, she'd be there with him every step of the way. Thankfully, though, her son had decided against it and Rachael had been grateful.

'Get through clinic,' she said out loud, and stood again, smoothing a hand down her skirt. Hopefully, she'd be able to finish with her patients and head home before or even *if* Joe came back to the clinic tonight. Then she would discuss the situation with Declan and together they'd figure how to deal with it.

Rachael headed out to the waiting room. 'Uh, Helen,' she said softly. 'My son's due to finish school soon and as it's just down the road, I've told him to walk here. I was hoping he could just sit in the kitchen and do his homework until I'm done? That's what we did at the last practice I worked at and he won't bother anyone. Sorry, I forgot to mention it before.'

Helen smiled. 'It's understandable with the shock you've had.'

'Thanks.'

'Is he all right to walk here by himself?'

'Sure.'

'He's not too young to be walking along a major road unsupervised?'

Rachael smiled nervously and cleared her throat, hoping

Helen wouldn't connect the dots too quickly. 'Oh, he's not little. Taller than me, in fact.'

'Oh. OK. Do you want me to let you know when he arrives?'

'Thanks. I'd appreciate it.' She turned and picked up her next patient's file. 'Mrs Gibson.' Rachael waited while her patient closed the magazine she was reading and levered herself up from the chair.

'Oof. It's getting harder every day to stand up.'

'I remember the feeling. Come this way.' Rachael's patient list had been mainly made up of women requiring their pregnancy or baby checks. She'd had several toddlers in as well and realised that her predecessor, Alison, had obviously taken all the 'family' cases. That didn't surprise her, knowing how Joe had never been interested in children and had declared he never planned to father any. If only he knew. She focused on her patient.

'I overheard you telling Helen you have a son. Was he a big baby?'

'Ten pounds seven ounces and one week early.'

'Ouch. I'm sorry I asked.'

Rachael led Mrs Gibson into her consulting room. 'Why don't you climb up onto the examination bed first to save any unnecessary moving around?' She helped her patient up. 'Is this your first child?'

'Third.'

'Sorry. I haven't had time to look at your notes.'

'That's all right. I'm sure there have been quite a few of us parading through here today. We'd all sit and chat in the waiting room and when Alison finished her day, we'd sometimes meet at the local coffee shop to complain about the frequent trips to the toilet and indigestion.'

Rachael laughed. 'I remember. It was a long time ago but, yes, I remember.'

'Just the one?'

'Yes.' Rachael pulled out the foetal heart monitor and together they listened to the baby's heartbeat. 'Perfect.'

'You didn't want to have any more?'

'I was very young when I had my son, and after he was born I was in medical school and then working.'

'You must have a very understanding husband,' Mrs Gibson said.

'Do you have any pain?' Rachael neatly avoided responding to the other woman's statement. Over the years, she'd found it easier to keep the wedding ring Joe had placed on her finger exactly where it was. Being a single mother had opened her up to all sorts of criticism and speculation from strangers. As Joe had taken care of completely battering her self-confidence, she hadn't needed anyone else's help to make her feel worthless.

Through medical school, after graduating and working extremely long hours at the hospital, she'd found the wedding ring afforded her some space from her colleagues as well as any unwanted attention.

Most importantly, though…she hadn't been able to take it off. Now she was so used to wearing it, she often forgot about it.

'No, no pain.'

'You're currently…' Rachael reached for the file '…thirty-six weeks? Is that right?'

'Well, you know, give or take a week.'

Rachael nodded. 'Have you had a show?'

'No. I didn't with my other two either.'

'OK.' Rachael helped Mrs Gibson to sit up. 'Were your other two early or late?'

'Late. Both of them, and they still are. We're always the last ones to leave places because the boys take so long to get their things together. Always the last to leave school because they just have to have one more go on the slippery-slip.'

Rachael smiled. 'I feel as though I've had a trip down

memory lane today. Now I'm used to endless hours of home-work and pimple creams in the bathroom.'

'Oh, stop.' Mrs Gibson covered her ears. 'I don't want to know.' The two women laughed.

'Everything looks fine, Mrs Gibson.'

'Wendy, please.'

Rachael nodded and smiled. 'I'll see you next week, if not before.'

'Oh, this one will be late, just like the other two, and, be-sides, I've got so much to get done before the baby's allowed to come.'

'If you say so, Wendy, but contact me if you have any questions, although I'm sure you know the drill.'

'Well and truly.'

Rachael wrote up the notes after Wendy had left, before going to get her final patient. It was four o'clock on the dot and she thought Declan should have been here by now. Then again, he'd probably stopped at the school library for some books. She forced herself not to worry.

'Bobby Rainer.' There was only one woman with a pram in the waiting room, a screaming baby inside, and Rachael motioned for them to come through.

'Take a seat,' she offered, as she sat behind her desk and checked the name of Bobby's mother. 'Tracy. What can I help you with today?'

'Can't you tell? Isn't it obvious?' The distraught young mother indicated the baby in the pram as she rocked it back and forth. 'Bobby isn't sleeping. It doesn't matter what I do, I can't get him to sleep at all. He just keeps crying.'

'OK.' Rachael stood up and went around to peer in the pram. 'When did you feed him last?'

'Just before we came.'

'He's your first?'

'And last, at this rate.' She sighed. 'That makes me sound like a terrible mother.'

'No.' Rachael smiled. 'It's quite understandable to feel that way, especially when you're probably not getting much sleep yourself. Mind if I pick him up?'

'Be my guest.'

Bobby didn't stop crying immediately when Rachael picked him up and she was silently pleased about that. If he had, it might have made Tracy feel worse. 'OK, OK, calm down, mister. It's all right,' she soothed. 'Does he usually quieten down when you pick him up?'

'Eventually, but I've been doing everything the nurses in hospital told me to do.'

'How old is he now?'

'Four weeks.'

'Feel longer?' Rachael smiled as she asked the question.

'Yes. I'm just so tired and I can't sleep and I'm for ever getting up to him, and my husband's been out of town on business for the past week and it's just got worse.' Tears sprang into her eyes and she took a tissue from a box on Rachael's desk and blew her nose. 'I just can't cope and on top of it all I have my nosy mother-in-law hanging around, telling me what I'm doing wrong and how none of her children ever cried like this. I feel so useless.'

As Tracy began to cry, Bobby began to settle.

Rachael waited a moment before saying, 'I know how you feel.'

'You do?' Tracy looked up in surprise.

'Well, not about the mother-in-law but about being tired and feeling as though you can't cope. I was only eighteen when I had my son. I was at a loss about exactly what I was supposed to do and how to settle him and when to put him down for a sleep and when to feed him.'

Tracy blew her nose. 'I can handle a boardroom full of cantankerous old men, I can prepare documents, write reviews, organise functions, but can I handle my own son? No.' She shook her head. 'It's just that they go through all the steps and what to do so quickly in the hospital, and the nurses are there to help you and then they just send you home and it's as though some maternal gene is supposed to click on and mine hasn't and I don't know what to do,' Tracy wailed, and started to cry again. 'And he cries and he's always hungry and then when he sleeps, I'm trying to get all the things done I need to do but he wakes up and...' she shook her head '...it doesn't work. I'm a failure as a mother.' Another fresh bout of tears followed and little Bobby joined in.

'What sort of help do you have?'

'Help? What help?'

'Friends? Family?'

'My parents are overseas and none of my friends have kids.'

'What about your mother-in-law?'

'I'd hardly call her a help. All she wants to do is criticise me.'

'Will your husband be away for long?'

'He's due back on Friday but I'm at the end, Dr Cusack. I need to do something. I can't take Bobby's screaming any more.' Tracy looked at her imploringly. 'What did you do? Tell me how you coped.'

'I was living at home with my parents. My mum was fantastic. She didn't take over but instead showed me the best way to do things. I honestly wouldn't have coped if it hadn't been for her.'

'You were lucky.'

'Yes.' Bobby had quietened down again, snuffling a little. 'Let's take a look at you, mister.' She carefully placed the baby on the examination couch, one hand holding him as his arms and legs squirmed. The instant he was supine again, he began to scream. She quickly felt his tummy, looked at his eyes, ears, nose and throat, but apart from noticing he was uptight about something, she couldn't see anything wrong.

She undid his clothes and checked him for rashes but found nothing.

Rachael picked him up again, this time holding him more upright as she patted his back and soothed him.

'Well? What's wrong with him?'

Rachael walked back towards Tracy as she kept rubbing Bobby's back. His crying had settled again and once more he sniffled. She rubbed her cheek on his soft, downy head, loving the feel. 'Babies cry for many reasons. They're hungry, need a nappy change, have wind, are too hot or too cold, over-stimulated, overtired or even because they're bored.'

'Bored? He's only one month old!'

Rachael smiled reassuringly. 'Yes, bored. He's a male, after all.'

Rachael's sexist comment managed to raise a smile from Tracy. 'True.' She blew her nose and put the tissues in the bin.

'Does he spit up little bits of milk after a feed? When you burp him?'

'Yes, all the time. He sometimes even vomits and then I have to start all over again.'

Rachael nodded. 'Bobby has reflux.'

'What's that?'

'After he's had a feed, when you lie him down on his back, some of the milk mixed with stomach acid comes back up. In essence, it's burning his throat.'

Tracy just stared at her son. 'So something is wrong?'

'Yes.'

'It's not just me?'

'No,' Rachael said softly.

'I'm not a bad mum?'

'No.'

'My poor baby.' A fresh bout of tears misted her eyes. 'Look at me. I can't stop crying.'

'It's quite normal, I'm afraid,' Rachael said with a smile.

'I'm so tired and I'm hardly sleeping and I can feel myself getting angry with him.' Tracy stopped, a guilty look crossing her face.

'You're afraid you're going to hurt him.' Rachael said the words she knew were on the tip of Tracy's tongue.

'I've heard stories about mothers shaking their babies and I used to think it was so cruel and that they should use more self-restraint but…' She shook her head. 'I'm there! I felt like shaking him last night and it scared me to death. That's why I came here today.'

Rachael stopped patting Bobby's back and placed her hand on Tracy's shoulder. 'You did the right thing and I'm proud of you. You're a good mother—and make sure you keep telling yourself that.'

Tracy's smile was heartfelt as she hiccuped a sigh. 'Thanks.'

Bobby had started to settle and was now just making a low groaning noise. Rachael could feel him getting heavier as he rested his head against her shoulder and realised he must be starting to go to sleep. 'Tell me about your day. I know you probably feel as though you're on a merry-go-round but just start somewhere.'

'I feed him, I change him, I burp him—just like the nurses showed me. I try to put him in his cot or on a rug on the floor while I either do the dishes or have something to eat or put the washing on. There's *so* much washing.'

'The washing is *always* there,' Rachael agreed. 'What then? Does he let you leave him?'

'Most of the times he screams and screams, so much that it scares me if I don't pick him up. I check his nappy again, I see if he has wind but he just doesn't settle.'

Rachael could see the anguish in Tracy's face. 'Go on.'

'So I pick him up and end up doing everything one-handed. It takes me for ever to hang up the washing.'

'Have you thought about a sling?'

'A sling?'

'A baby sling. You can put Bobby in the sling, which you wear around you, and then you have both hands free.'

'A sling.' Tracy nodded as though it were the most startling revelation she'd ever heard.

'That only gives you a hands-free option for a while. Keep going. What happens next?'

'It just starts all over again. The feeding, the changing, the burping, the not settling.'

Bobby was now asleep in her arms and Rachael found herself quite content to hold him for a bit longer. Besides, they needed to adjust the pram before he was put back in.

'He cries.'

'Does he seem to be feeding well? Getting enough food? Does he cry for more when he's finished?'

'No. The only time he's quiet is when he's drinking.'

'So you just snatch food whenever you can.'

'Yes. I'm tired and exhausted. I'm up most of the night with him. I'm dead on my feet.'

'You need more sleep.'

'How? I can't wait until Friday when Paul comes home.'

'I'm not suggesting you do. I know this is probably going to drive you crazy, but what about asking your mother-in-law to look after Bobby tomorrow? Just for a few hours so you can get some sleep. Is he her only grandchild?'

'Yes.'

'Then she obviously wants to be involved. Asking her to help in this way may actually serve two purposes. First, it will get her off your back with all her…er…shall we say rather helpful suggestions and, secondly, you get some quality time to sleep.'

'But—'

'Is his cot in your bedroom?'

'No.'

'Bring it in, at least for the next two nights.'

'But all the books say—'

'Let's forget about the books for the moment. Sometimes you need to go with what works. It's not going to be for ever—just a few nights. Your husband isn't home so it would just be you and Bobby. Have the cot by or close to the bed so you don't have to go far to get to him. When you feed him, try and keep him as upright as possible. Use pillows to prop you both up and once you've fed and burped him, give him a bit of antacid.' Rachael named a brand and told Tracy how much to give him. 'I'll give you a medicine syringe so you can measure out the exact dosage. Then you just gently squeeze it into his mouth.'

'And that's it?'

'Try that for the next two nights and see how he settles. You'll need to elevate his cot mattress by putting a pillow underneath it—the same with his pram. Can you raise the back part of the pram so he's sitting more upright rather than lying down?'

Tracy fiddled with the pram for a moment before adjusting it as Rachael had suggested.

'When he's upright, there's less chance of reflux occurring. Giving him the antacid will help soothe the burning he feels, and I wouldn't be at all surprised if you get more sleep to-night.'

'Good. Do I really need to call my mother-in-law?'

Rachael smiled. 'I'd strongly suggest it. If you can get two hours of uninterrupted sleep tomorrow as well as a good sleep tonight, you'll be feeling like a new woman by Wednesday, which is when I want you to come and see me again.'

'Thank you, Dr Cusack. I really mean it. You've made me feel as though I'm a person again.' Tracy laughed. 'That sounds silly.'

'No. It sounds quite logical. I'll walk you out.' Rachael opened the door, still holding little Bobby in her arms. She rubbed her cheek on his head once more and gave him a kiss. 'Thank you for letting me cuddle him.'

Helen cooed and clucked at the sleeping baby as she made another appointment for Tracy. The outside door opened and Declan walked in just as Rachael was settling Bobby into his pram.

'Hi, handsome man.' She turned to Tracy. 'This is what they grow up to be. They continually eat and there's still a lot of washing to do.'

Tracy laughed and Rachael was glad to see a different woman emerge from her consulting room to the one who had gone in. 'See you on Wednesday.'

Declan held the door for Tracy and Rachael was proud of her son's manners and thoughtfulness. Once her patient had gone, he came over and slung his arm about her shoulders. She hugged him close, breathing in his familiar scent, her heart filling with love. 'How was today?'

'OK. You finished yet?'

'Yes. You're a little later than I expected.'

'Stopped by the library.' He jerked a thumb towards his backpack.

'I thought you might. I'll get my things and we can go.' She turned and caught Helen staring at Declan. 'Oh, sorry. I forgot to introduce you. Helen, this is my son, Declan.'

Helen stared in stunned disbelief, her jaw slack.

There was a sound from the back of the house and a door could be heard closing. Muffled footsteps sounded up the carpeted corridor.

'Helen?' Joe was getting closer. 'Did I leave the file on—?' He stopped as he came into the waiting room and saw Rachael. 'Uh…hi.' Then he looked at the person by her side. Rachael dropped her arm from around Declan's waist and clenched her hands tightly in an effort to control the feeling of dread that swamped her.

Rachael watched as Joe looked the boy up and down before slowly shaking his head.

'Er…Joe.' She cleared her throat and forced the words out. 'I'd like you to meet Declan. My son.'

'Joe?' Declan said, and Rachael turned to look up at him. She nodded. '*The* Joe?'

Rachael nodded again.

'My *dad Joe*?'

Rachael glanced at her son, then Helen and finally to Joe. 'Yes.'

CHAPTER TWO

SHE watched as Joe swallowed, once…twice, his gaze never leaving Declan.

Helen was the first to break the silence. 'Well, there's no point in getting a paternity test to confirm this. You're the dead spit of your father when he was your age.'

'You knew him back then?' Declan looked at the woman behind the receptionist's desk.

Helen smiled. 'I've known your father since he was about twelve years old. I may even have a photograph of him somewhere at home.'

'Cool.'

'I'll see if I can find it for you. For now, though, why don't you come through to the kitchen and I'll get you a drink?'

Rachael glanced at Helen, giving her a smile of thanks. Joe barely moved as Helen led Declan past him, but his blue gaze swung to her, pinning her to the spot. It was the exact same look he'd given her the morning they'd signed the annulment papers. Knowing she needed her wits about her, she physically pulled herself up to her full height of five feet eight, and with the added two inches from her shoes, she mentally felt more in control. Smoothing a hand down her skirt to get the perspiration off her hands, she took a breath and indicated to the empty waiting-room chairs.

'Please, sit down, Joe. This can't be easy for you.' Thank goodness her voice sounded natural and calm.

'Don't, Rachael. Don't be the polite, well-bred debutante you were raised to be. It doesn't work in this situation.'

'That's an unfair crack, Joe. I just thought it might be easier to discuss this sitting down.'

'How…civilised. Well, you know me of old, Rach, I'm not a civilised type of guy.'

'What? Going to punch me out?'

'I don't hit women.'

'No, you just break their hearts.'

Joe opened his mouth to say she'd done the same thing to him but stopped. Raking a hand through his hair, he tried to get some sort of control over the shock he'd just received.

'Helen's right. Why bother with a paternity test when the kid looks just like me?'

'Declan. His name is Declan.'

'Declan what? What's his surname, Rach?'

'Cusack.'

'Not Silvermark? Why? Didn't want him following in his father's footsteps?'

'Look, Joe, you made it quite clear you never wanted to have children the day we annulled our marriage. In fact, wasn't that one of the reasons you cited to get the marriage annulled? I wanted children and you didn't, so we were at an impasse?'

'*We* cited.'

'No, Joe. *You*. You were the one who pushed for it.'

'You went along with it.'

'What choice did I have? The man I'd not only fallen head over heels in love with *and* married told me two days later it had all been a joke just to get me into bed. You'd completely humiliated me and broken my heart in the process. You wanted to be rid of me so I let you, but don't go trying to blame our failed relationship on me. At least I was willing to work at it.'

She was right. She had been more than willing to work things out. She'd told him she could do without ever having children but he'd seen in her eyes that she'd been lying. He closed his eyes for a moment, trying to deal with the situation better than he had all those years ago. She'd ended up begging him and she had no idea just how hard it had been for him to walk away. He'd *had* to hurt her, he'd *had* to push her away because back then he'd loved her too much to ruin her life.

'It wouldn't have mattered how much we'd worked at it, Rach, it would have ended in misery.' The words came out dejected and he hated her for hauling all these old emotions back to the surface. Earlier in the day when he'd decided he needed some sort of closure where Rachael was concerned, he hadn't expected the emotions to be so powerful. And now…now…to top everything off, he discovered he had a son.

'Why didn't you tell me about the boy?'

'Would you have listened to me? Believed me? Wanted us back?' He remained silent and she saw the answer right there in his face. 'You'd already said anything between us was doomed to failure. Do you honestly believe that was something I'd do to my son?'

'*Our* son.'

'Oh, so you want one now, do you?'

He ground his teeth together. 'My opinion on children hasn't changed but, regardless of that, I won't deny Declan is mine.'

'How magnanimous of you. Well, for your information, Declan and I are doing just fine and we have for the past fourteen years.'

He deserved that but it was yet another kick in the stomach. 'Is this why you didn't want to stay here at the clinic? Because you were afraid I'd discover the truth about him?'

'No.'

'Wait a minute.' Joe's thoughts began to catch up with him. 'Declan knew my name.'

'Yes.'

'He knows about me?' he asked incredulously.

'I've never lied to him.'

'So he's known about me all along?'

'Yes.'

'Isn't that a bit tough for a young kid to take?'

'I didn't tell him everything the instant he was born, Joe, but neither did I hide the truth. As he's grown older, we've discussed it in more detail. I've always told him that if he ever wanted to find you I would help him, but he decided against it.'

'Probably just as well,' Joe mumbled, but she heard him.

'It's quite clear you don't want either of us in your life, Joe, and that's not a problem. I've agreed to stay here until the end of next week, which gives Helen sufficient time to find another locum to cover the rest of Alison's maternity leave. Once that's over, Declan and I will be out of your life for ever.'

'And if Declan wants to get to know me?'

Rachael frowned, her tone changing. 'I won't have him hurt, Joe. If he does then you have a decision to make. You're either in or you're out because I won't have him messed about.'

'But I'm his father.'

'No.' She hardened her heart against him. She would some-how find a way to cope with the emotions he was evoking within her, but where Declan was concerned she refused point blank to have her son hurt. She'd go head to head with her stubborn ex-husband if she had to. 'You've never been his father, Joe. In fact, you were nothing more than the sperm donor.'

She certainly knew how to cut him to the quick and he tried not to wince at her words. 'Does that mean you were planning to trap me by getting pregnant?'

'Trap you? Trap you with what? Marriage? We were al-ready married, Joe. We didn't have sex until our wedding night. What type of trap are you talking about? Besides, why on earth would I plan to get pregnant at the age of eighteen when I was all set to go to medical school?'

She was right. He wasn't thinking straight. How could he? 'You obviously made it.'

'I was forced to learn at an early age how to survive.' She lifted her chin with a hint of defiance. 'Now, if you'll excuse me, Declan and I have an appointment.'

'Where?'

'It's none of your business, Joe.'

She was right—again. She headed towards him and stopped when there were only inches between them. 'You have a decision to make. You're either willing to get to know him or you're not. Make the choice and let me know your decision. Until then, Declan is off limits.'

'Protecting the young?'

'I'm his mother.' The words were said with pride and confidence. He could tell from the look in her icy-cold blue eyes that she meant business. It was a warning as well as a threat, and Joe nodded sharply, acknowledging her words. He hated it when she was right, and he knew she was. It wasn't fair to the kid. Rachael had always been a straightshooter. She said what she thought and that had been one of the things that had attracted him to her in the first place. OK, the first had been her looks and gorgeous body, but her directness and honesty had been highly important to him, given his past.

Joe couldn't help looking over his shoulder as she stalked down the corridor. Her back was straight, her hips wiggled in that innocent yet provocative way and her skirt, which came to just above the knee, revealed a good portion of those luscious legs he'd coveted all those years ago.

A low, guttural sound of desire rumbled in his throat and he forced himself to look away. He still wanted her. Was that a good sign? Surely it couldn't be a healthy sign! He was looking for closure, not to start anything up with her again.

He headed into his consulting room and shut the door, not

wanting to see Rachael and her son—*their* son, he corrected himself as they left. For the first time in fourteen years he wanted a drink. Something smooth and calming—like brandy—to wash away the pain. Or perhaps a few quick shots of tequila to help him forget. But he'd given up drinking after that fateful day on Waikiki beach.

'Where did he go?' Joe heard Declan ask, and held his breath, waiting for his consulting-room door to open. Rachael's muted tones followed and a moment later he heard them leave. He walked around to his desk, knowing Helen would be pouncing on him at any second, and he just wanted another moment's peace to try desperately to get himself together.

There was a brief knock at the door, then Helen entered. 'Mind if I come in?'

'If I say no, will you go away?' he asked rhetorically. 'I'm actually surprised you knocked. Usually you just barge right in.'

'Except when you have patients with you.' He acknowledged her words with a nod while he waited for Helen to seat herself in the chair opposite him. 'Do you think there are any more shocks still to come?' she asked.

'With Rachael? No doubt.'

'Is that a fair statement? Because from everything you've told me about your extremely brief marriage to the woman, it sounds as though she wasn't at fault for any of it. You can hardly blame her for not telling you about the boy.'

'Hey, whose side are you on?'

'Hers.'

'Thanks. I thought you were my friend.'

Helen had the audacity to laugh. She walked around and leant against his desk, placing a maternal hand on his shoulder. 'I couldn't have children, Joe. You've always known that, and for some reason when I met you at the hospital when you were brought in at the age of twelve for your first set of stitches, well for some strange reason I took a liking to you. I thought to myself, Helen, old girl, here is a kid who's good at heart and with a little love and kindness will make a real difference in the world.' She paused and moved her hand to cup his cheek. 'Of course I'm your friend, Joe. I love you like a son and I'm proud of everything you've accomplished. You've pulled yourself up from the depths of the gutter and made a success of your life.'

'Why do I feel there's a "but" coming?'

'Because there is, Declan. I only spent a few minutes with him, Joe, but he's a good kid. A *smart* kid. He's going to that co-ed school down the road.'

'The one for gifted children?'

'Yes. He told me he was successful in getting a place there—and, believe me, they don't accept new candidates lightly. Rachael quit her practice in Cairns to move here for him.'

Joe nodded. 'Sounds like a Rachael thing to do.'

'You told me once that you trusted her. You're not a man to trust easily, Joe, so when you give your trust to someone, it's like a rare and very precious gift.' Helen paused, watching him closely. 'I know you've only spent a brief amount of time with both of them, but do you trust her with Declan?'

'That's a strange question. How should I know?'

'You're looking at it from a worldly angle. I'm asking about your gut instincts, your heart and soul. Do you trust her with Declan?'

Joe thought for a moment, remembering that protective look she'd levelled him with. A mother protecting her chick. 'Yes.'

'Would you trust yourself with him?'

Again Joe thought. He was on Helen's wavelength now and he felt a lot of the emotions he'd fought off as a child beginning to return. 'I never asked to be a father.' The words came out choked. He remembered hearing those same words come

out of his own father's mouth when his mother had been
pregnant with his baby brother. *I never asked to be a father!*
The words had been hurtled abusively, along with a few slaps
across his mother's face. Both of them had been drunk but at
the time he hadn't realised that. All he'd known at the age of
four had been the feeling of total rejection and utter fear. 'I
didn't want to be a father.'

'But you are.' Helen's tone was firm.

'I'm no good at this stuff. Caring for people. Playing happy
families. It's just not me. I'll stuff it up, just like my old man
did.'

'What utter garbage, and I personally resent it. You are
nothing like your old man or any of those other jerks your
mother hooked up with. You are more than capable of caring
for people. Just look at Melina and myself.'

'Melina's my half-sister and you're different.'

'How?'

'You're *you*.' Joe raked a hand through his hair. 'You know
what I mean.'

'Yes, I do, and that's my point. I know you care for me,
Joe, and you have done for almost twenty years.'

He smiled, trying to lighten the moment. 'Has it been that
long?'

'Declan is a part of you.' Helen's words were soft but imploring and Joe's smile disappeared. 'Your blood runs through
him. No, you didn't ask for it but it's happened. Accept it and
think about his life. You didn't know about him before but
you do now and the decisions you make will have long-lasting
repercussions.' Helen's gaze softened. 'He seems like a good
kid, and he was so excited to finally get to meet you.' She
paused. 'Don't mess with him, Joe. At the very least, you owe
him that.'

His pager beeped and he glanced at the number. 'They need
me back on set.'

Helen nodded and moved away from him. 'Go. Work. Think. I'll lock up.'

Joe waited until she'd left his room before taking a deep breath. He could feel the dark clouds beginning to close in on him once more and he hated that feeling. Move. Move! He needed to keep busy, to get to the studio where he could immerse himself in the intricacies involved in movie-making.

The studio wasn't far and Joe, who felt like just driving his car far out of town until it ran out of petrol, forced himself to slow down and obey the road rules. He tried not to think about Rachael or Declan while he worked, but found it almost impossible. Dark thoughts, distant memories from his childhood kept raising their ugly heads. His father hitting his mother, his father hitting him, his father walking out the door. The losers his mother had hooked up with after that… One by one he recalled their faces, surprised at how the boxes he'd thought firmly locked in his subconscious opened easily with little prompting.

The babies his mother had had. For a while there she'd seemed to be constantly pregnant and always by a different guy. Joe shook his head, almost desperate to get the lids back on those boxes and push them back into the shadows where they belonged. He couldn't be a father. He refused to take responsibility for wrecking Declan's life, as he knew he would. It was genetic. His old man had been a loser and Joe had worked long and hard…struggled and scraped…to get himself to where he was. He'd taken a stand and refused to ruin his life, but when it came to the paternal instinct, he doubted he had one.

After two hours on the set, watching the actors do a fight sequence over and over, Joe checked their limbs for new bruises and any circulatory problems before pronouncing them both fine to go home and rest in a bath full of ice.

With his job done, he was free to head home…but home meant being alone with his thoughts and that was the last thing he wanted right now. Joe walked over to Wong, the stunt coordinator. 'Anyone booked in the training room tonight?' he asked his friend.

'No.' Wong peered closely at him. 'You don't look so good. Lots of anger around your eyes. Bad day, Joe?'

Had it been bad? No, not bad, just mind-tilting. 'I've had worse.'

Wong laughed. 'I'll bet. You want some help in the training room?'

'Yeah. That'd be great.'

'OK. Get changed, I'll meet you there.'

Joe headed to his car and pulled out a bag. It was an old habit he doubted he'd ever get out of as it contained all the essentials—toothbrush, clean clothes, shaver and brush, as well as a pair of sweats for times like these. When a kid lived on the streets, he learned to pack light and pack well. Joe had lived like that for many years, with one bag containing all his major possessions in the world. Then he'd gone to America…and met Rachael. For the first time, he'd experienced a 'possession' he couldn't fit into a bag.

He let Wong strap his hands before fitting the boxing gloves on top. Joe eyed the bag that hung from the low ceiling which was just waiting for his frustrations to be pounded into it. He thought about Rachael, about Declan, about how his world had just completely changed. He tapped the bag, gently testing but also not wanting to think about her when he was pummelling out his anger. She hadn't done anything wrong. He'd been the one who'd pushed her away, who'd wanted her out of his life. He couldn't blame her for not telling him about Declan.

He could, however, blame his mother. His father. His numerous stepfathers. The welfare system. The teachers at school. The kids who had taunted him and his brother. His brother, John. John, who had followed in his big brother's footsteps and become involved with street gangs. Joe had managed to get out of them in the end but John had died and Joe held himself responsible. He began to hit the bag with more effort and soon was pounding out his ghosts, wanting them gone from his life for ever.

He had no idea how long he'd pounded the bag but when Wong told him to slow down or he'd do himself an injury, Joe did as he was told. When they took off the gloves, the strapping around his knuckles was tinged red with blood.

'Maybe I should have stopped you sooner.' Wong undid the strapping and told him to go and shower. 'Come back tomorrow. You still have lots of aggression left.'

Joe nodded and thanked his friend before heading to the showers. He let the water wash over him and although he felt weary and tired, his mind was still active with questions. Questions he wanted…no, *needed* answers to. There was no way he was going to sleep tonight, even after the workout, until he could get his head around what had happened today.

After he'd changed, he headed back to the clinic. Turning the alarm off, he riffled through the filing cabinet, looking for the file on Rachael. He pulled it out and noted her address, surprised to discover she was staying in a hotel. He grabbed his keys, switched off the lights and reset the alarm before driving to the address.

With determination in every step, he left the hotel lift and strode down the corridor to the room listed in her file at his medical practice. He knocked, and when she opened the door he tried not to gasp. He also tried to control the twisting of desire in his gut, but it was impossible.

Her dark, wet hair was hanging loosely around her shoulders, contrasting with the white hotel robe belted at her waist. He'd seen her looking like that before and his memory was as clear as though it had been only yesterday…only yesterday when he'd removed the robe and taken his sweet time making love to his wife.

'Oh,' she gasped, a blush tinging her cheeks. She looked him up and down, the blush deepening. Nervously, Rachael swallowed. 'Joe. Uh…I was expecting room service.'

Joe forced his mind to clear. 'Look, Rach, I know you told me to decide about Declan but I can't do that without more information.'

He watched as she switched into protective mother mode. 'What sort of information?'

'Can I see him?'

'He's not here.'

Joe hadn't expected that. 'Where is he?'

'He's gone out with my parents to choose a new place for us to live.'

'But it's almost eight o'clock.'

'And?' She waited. 'What's that supposed to mean?'

'Er… I don't know. Doesn't he have homework? Need to be in bed or something?'

She laughed. 'He's almost fifteen, Joe, not five.'

He could feel her softening and took advantage of the situation. 'Can I come in? Please, Rach? Just for a few minutes. My mind is in a spin.'

She glanced down at her robe, then stepped back from the door. 'OK.' When he walked into the room, it seemed to shrink with his overwhelming presence.

'Nice room.' He waved his arm absently around the space, and she caught a glimpse of his hand. The knuckles were red, cut and bruised.

'What have you done?' Without thinking, she crossed to his side and lifted one hand in hers. Joe jerked back instantly. 'What did you do?'

'Nothing. I was working out.' He tried to control himself but her touch had burned him and her fresh, clean, scent was starting to overpower him. She smelt so good.

'On who?'

'Uncalled for, Rach.'

'Yes. Sorry.'

'I was working out on a punching bag.'

'Oh. It's none of my business. I'm sorry. I'll just get dressed.'

'No need to bother on my account.' The words were out before he could stop them.

'Joe!' The blush grew even deeper, her eyes wide and round with surprise.

'Sorry. That was way out of line.'

'Yes. I guess we're even now.' She snatched up a handful of clothes and headed for the bathroom. Joe wondered what she'd do if he followed her and kissed her the way he had in the past. She'd probably throw him out and again he acknowledged she'd have every right to, but he had to admit that the attraction between the two of them was as potent as ever. He'd never been one to believe in love at first sight. He was too cynical, too wise to the ways of the world yet—bam! It had hit him like a ton of bricks the first time he'd set eyes on Rachael.

A few minutes later she came out the bathroom dressed, a white towel around her shoulders as she rubbed the ends of her hair. He'd seen her do this before and again he had to force the memories not to intrude. He was here with the purpose of getting answers, and that was exactly what he was going to do.

Joe looked out the window at the ocean view. There were other high-rise apartments and hotels to the left and right but she'd scored a great room with a relaxing view of the ocean. If he looked out the window, it meant he didn't have to look at Rachael. She was too distracting.

'So, what do you want to know?'

'Why you didn't tell me?'

'I tried, Joe.' He turned at her words.

'And that means?'

'I tried to find you.' Rachael sighed and hung the towel

over the back of a chair. She bit her lip, watching him closely.
'After I returned home from the trip…I wasn't well. At first
I thought it was just heartbreak.' She saw him wince. 'You
wanted the truth, Joe, and I hope you still believe that with
me, that's what you'll always get.'

He nodded but made no other comment.

'I didn't find out until I was four months pregnant. My
body was so out of whack, what with travelling and then
being so miserable when I returned. After four months my
mother forced me to go to the doctor for a check-up, and
that's when I found out.'

'That must have impressed your parents.'

She laughed without humour. 'You have no idea. Until
then, I hadn't told them about you. They'd known something
had been wrong when I'd returned, but thankfully they hadn't
pressured me about it. Now, though, there was a grandchild
on the way and the whole ball game changed. So I went to
Brisbane to find you.'

'Even though you knew how I felt about children?'

'Yes. You had a right to know, Joe.'

'Yet you didn't find me.'

'You obviously didn't want to be found,' she countered. 'I
didn't have much to go on and I had morning sickness
throughout my entire pregnancy. By the end of the seventh
month, I had pre-eclampsia and my doctor put me in hospital
until Declan was born. Anyway, I knew you had lived in
Brisbane and which suburb you were raised in, but that was
all I had to go on. Finding where you lived was like looking
for a needle in a haystack, but I eventually found your
mother's house.'

Joe was shocked. 'You spoke to my mother?'

'Yes.'

'Did you tell her about the baby?'

'No. I merely told her I was looking for you.'

Joe turned away from her, unable to believe she'd seen the

dive where he'd grown up. In the poorest part of Brisbane, the government weatherboard house falling down around itself. The front yard littered with broken toys, bits of cars and general junk. He felt sick thinking she'd seen that side of his life, the side he'd wanted to protect her from.

'How did she react?'

'She said she hadn't heard from you in over six months and that the money you usually sent had stopped coming. Joe, she thought you'd probably died.'

'She said that?' He looked at Rachael once more.

'In a manner of speaking, yes.'

Joe knew she was giving him the 'cleaned up' version of the story. Knowing his mother, she'd have taken one look at Rachael and tried to figure out how much money she could get out of her. Even now, standing barefoot in a hotel room, she looked as though she'd stepped from a glossy magazine. The denim jeans were designer label, the powder blue top was the latest fashion. Her clothes spoke of style and money. They always had, but he also knew that clothes didn't make the woman.

Rachael had always carried herself well. Her walk was determined, sure and purposeful. Even when she'd been eighteen, she'd had such purpose about her, and Joe had coveted it, wanting to have the confidence that exuded from her.

He was watching her again, the way he had when they'd first met. She'd always thought he'd looked at her as though he'd unwrapped a big, shiny package and wasn't quite sure what to do with it. Warmth spread through her and she felt the stirrings of repressed desire beginning to sizzle once more. How could he do that to her with just one look?

He'd always been able to make her go weak at the knees and today he'd done it several times. He was dressed in his staple outfit of blue denims and a white T-shirt. All that was missing was the well-worn leather jacket, and he'd be a dead ringer for the instant she'd first laid eyes on him. They stared at each other.

Rachael swallowed nervously, her tongue darting out to wet her lips. Joe groaned as he watched the action and closed his eyes tight. His hands were by his side, also clenched tight as he fought the attraction bubbling between them.

'Did you believe her?' The words were ground out as he finally achieved his goal and opened his eyes. Rachael turned away and crossed to the bedside table to pick up a comb. Slowly she began to pull it through her dark locks.

'Hmm?'

'My mother. When she said I was dead. Did you believe her?'

Rachael remembered the scene as though it had been yesterday. Her heart had stopped for one moment before she'd instinctively known it hadn't been true. 'No.'

'Did you give her any money?'

'Joe, I don't think this is—'

'Did you give her money?' he demanded.

'Yes, but it wasn't a lot. About eighty dollars.'

'That would have been enough. Did she ask for it?'

'No, but she kind of implied she needed it for your siblings.'

'*Half*-siblings.'

Rachael shrugged. 'Whatever.'

'She would have used that money to buy alcohol. You know that, don't you?'

'What? No. Surely she wouldn't. Those kids looked hungry.'

'We were always hungry.' Joe turned away once more. He'd been desperate to shield Rachael from his background, from the life of poverty he'd lived. She was too pure, too special, too loving to even have seen the squalor he'd been raised in.

He needed to move this on. His chest was starting to feel

tight, and the longer he remained in a room alone with her, the harder it was to control himself. He wanted to grab her, to crush her to him, to press his mouth firmly on hers and see whether the old spark really *was* still there or whether it was just his memory playing tricks on him.

'OK. So you saw my mother and she didn't know where I was, so then what?'

'Then I tried to remember everything we'd talked about and I realised how little you'd told me about yourself. Oh, I knew what made you laugh, what colour you liked...' She lowered her voice a little. '...How you took your coffee.' She shrugged. 'That sort of thing. But when it came to you and what you'd done before you'd met me, I drew a blank. I honestly didn't know where to look, Joe. I put an ad in the Brisbane, Sydney and Melbourne papers for two months but got no response. I tried again a week or so before I had Declan but still no response. I was scared to be by myself, to be bringing a child into the world. I knew my parents were there to help and, believe me, they were incredible, but it wasn't the same.'

Rachael could feel tears beginning to threaten once more and turned away. 'Sorry. I should be over this by now.'

Joe wanted to go to her. To comfort her. To apologise for his callousness. But he knew that if he touched her, it would mean the end of all rational thought.

She wiped her eyes and took a deep breath, pulling herself together. 'Anyway, to answer your original question, I didn't tell you because I couldn't find you. It's as simple as that.'

'Rach.' He couldn't take it any longer. He covered the distance between them and put his hands on her shoulders. She shied away and Joe winced as though she'd slapped him. She turned to look at him.

'Don't, Joe. Don't touch me.'

'Why not?'

His words were barely audible, but even if he hadn't spoken

she could read the message clearly in his eyes. He was still attracted to her and she was sure he could see she reciprocated his feelings. He edged closer. 'Why not?'

'Joe.' Her heart was pounding fiercely against her chest, her breath coming out between her parted lips in shallow gasps. She shook her head as he moved even closer. 'Joe.' This time his name came out as a sigh and she realised her mind was quickly losing the battle to her body and she wanted nothing more than to have his arms wrapped firmly around her, their lips pressed hungrily together.

He trailed his fingers down her cheek, revelling in the smoothness of her skin. 'You're still so beautiful, Rach.' He buried his other hand in her hair, unable to believe he was touching her once more.

'Your skin is so soft.' He brushed his thumb across her lips and almost went to pieces when she gasped at the touch. He groaned and hauled her close, wanting to kiss her but at the same time not wanting to ignite something he wasn't sure he could control. He breathed in the scent of her hair. 'Your hair smells amazing.'

Rachael's eyelids fluttered closed and she clung to him, knowing she was passing the point of no return and not caring. She plunged her fingers into his hair, desperate to bring his head closer to her lips, to erase the agony of wanting him, which was gripping her entire body. 'Joe.' She whispered his name and slid her hands down to cup his face as she looked up into his eyes.

Something deep in the recesses of Joe's mind tugged at him. There was still something he needed to address and it was important. He raised one hand to where she touched him and pulled her left hand away from his face. He glanced down and saw the simple gold wedding band.

Helen had mentioned his new locum was married, but with everything else which had happened today, he'd completely forgotten.

'Joe?' Rachael looked at him in bewilderment. 'Joe? What's wrong?'

Joe let his arms drop and took a step back. 'What's wrong? Rachael—you're wearing a wedding ring!'

CHAPTER THREE

JOE turned away from her and stalked towards the door. 'How could you possibly have forgotten you were married?'

A million emotions flooded through Rachael in a matter of thirty seconds. She wanted to pull him back into her arms and tell him the ring was the same one he'd placed on her finger in that small Vegas chapel all those years ago. Another part of her wanted to hurt him as much as he'd hurt her and let him believe she was married to someone else.

But she'd always been an honest person and regardless of how Joe made her feel, whether it be sensually desirable or flaming mad, she'd always been truthful with him. However, if she confessed it was the ring he'd given her, she'd probably be opening herself up for more hurt in the near future. Two weeks. She only had to stay at his practice for two weeks and then she could move on.

Rachael cleared her throat and flipped her hair out of her face, her chin raised with a hint of defiance. He loved it when she looked like that but he forced himself to concentrate. What possible explanation was she going to give for wearing a wedding ring and falling apart in his arms the moment he'd touched her? The attraction was there between them, it was as strong as ever, but surely not so strong that she'd forget about the man she was married to?

'Joe, I'm not married.'

OK. That was the last thing he'd been expecting her to say. 'But the ring?' He pointed to her hand completely bewildered.

Rachael shrugged. 'I didn't like the stigmatism that went with being labelled a single mother. Nowadays it's a common occurrence but even fifteen years ago a woman pushing a pram without wearing a wedding ring was frowned on. Medical school would have been even more of a nightmare if I'd chosen not to wear the ring. Most of my professors were quite old-fashioned.'

He understood that. He'd had quite a few who, when they'd discovered his background, had told him to forget about medical school. He'd been riled by their comments and even more determined to prove their prejudices wrong.

'Thankfully, times have changed,' she continued.

'So why still wear it?'

She shrugged once more. 'I forget it's there most of the time.' There was a knock at the door. 'That'll be room service.'

'You're not eating with your son?'

'My parents wanted to take Declan out to dinner and then look at apartments. It was a special treat for him.'

'And you weren't invited?'

Rachael walked passed him to the door. 'They haven't seen him for six months and wanted some time alone with him.' She opened the door, thankful for the distraction. There was no way she was telling Joe she'd been unable to go out with her family tonight. The shock of the day had been too much for her to cope with and she hadn't been ready to answer her parents' questions about Joe.

She signed for the food and told the waiter she'd take care of setting it up.

'Thank you, Dr Cusack,' he said, before disappearing.

'I'll go and leave you to eat,' Joe muttered.

'You said you had questions and if you don't mind, I'd rather get them out the way before Declan returns. I want your decision, Joe. You're either in or out of his life and I need that information by tomorrow. Declan's already asking questions and getting excited.' She levelled a firm stare at Joe. 'I won't have him hurt.'

'I understand. All right.' He straightened his shoulders as

though he was getting ready for battle. 'Why did you move to the Gold Coast?' Helen had told him it was so Declan could go to that fancy school, but he wanted to hear if Rachael had a different reason. Had she known he lived here? Had she specifically chosen his practice to work at, hoping he might get to know his son?

'For Declan. He was accepted to a good school here.' She named the school and Joe nodded, as impressed as he'd been when Helen had told him.

'Wow. That school is almost impossible to get into. Isn't that a school for gifted children?'

'Yes, although I can't stand that label. Declan has a high IQ, and at the beginning of this term he was offered a place. It's all been rather sudden, hence the fact that we don't have anywhere to live. Still, I'd make any sacrifice for him.'

'High IQ, eh?' Joe felt like preening. His boy, *his son* was smart. He shook his head in bemusement.

'You're no dummy yourself, Joe. You just didn't have anyone to support you while you were growing up. If people tell you you're useless, after a while you begin to believe them.'

He hated it that she could read him so easily.

'This term isn't going to be easy for him. For a start, he's beginning in the second term while all the other new kids started at the beginning of the year. Also, a lot of these kids have been there since they started high school. Then there's the downside to being a smart kid.'

'What's that?'

'He suffers from anxiety. It can get quite bad sometimes, and when it does he doesn't eat, he doesn't sleep and, quite frankly, Joe, it's scary to see him going through it. Can't you see why I need an answer from you? I don't want him stressed out. I don't want him getting his hopes up about you, only to have them dashed when, after a few short weeks, you decide you don't want to play father any more.'

'That's a little unfair.'

'It's very unfair, Joe, but I need that decision. If you're in, then you're in for the rest of his life. Up until now you've had the excuse that you didn't know about him, but now you know.'

'You can't just dump this on me, Rachael. It's a lot to take in. This morning I got up, went to work and saw you. That was bad enough, but by this afternoon I'd discovered I was a father! Now you want me to choose? My whole life has been flipped in less than twenty-four hours.'

'You're thirty-four, Joe. I had all this dumped on me when I was eighteen! My husband didn't want me any more and a few months later I found out I was pregnant, so don't go putting this back on me. You're used to adapting, Joe. It's what you're good at. You adapted to the role of traveller when you set out to see the world. You adapted quickly to the role of friend, then boyfriend and finally husband—all within a matter of three weeks. Then you adapted even more quickly to the role of ex-husband and disappeared off the face of the earth. Don't go giving me speeches and platitudes. It doesn't matter whether or not you gel with Declan, it doesn't matter whether or not you can put up with me. You either want him in your life or you don't. Yes, your life has changed in the past twenty-four hours, but there's no going back. Your life has changed for ever. Now act like a grown-up and deal with it.'

The phone rang and she snatched it up. 'Yes?' Rachael turned away from Joe, forcing herself to take a deep breath.

'Dr Cusack? I'm the night manager. We have an emergency downstairs in the restaurant and need your help.' There was urgency and repressed panic in the man's tone.

'I'll be right there. Meet me at the lift.' Rachael hung up the phone and slipped on a pair of shoes. 'Emergency downstairs.' She grabbed the room key-card and headed out, knowing Joe would follow. He was a doctor and this was what

doctors did. They put their personal lives on hold when their
work required them to.

The instant the lift doors opened in the lobby, the night
manager was by their side. 'Over here. We've called the ambulance but this man isn't at all well.' He led them through
the dining room and out the back through to the staff corri-
dors. He opened a side door to reveal an elderly woman weep-
ing next to a man who had just been carried through by two
young waiters. The room was quite small and the staff had
pushed together two armchairs for the man to lie on.

'No!' Joe snapped authoritatively. 'Get him on the floor.'
The two waiters did as they were told. 'We'll take it from
here,' Joe said. 'Get me the hotel's medical kit, immediately.'

The night manager nodded and ordered one of the waiters
to find one. Rachael began to loosen the man's clothes while
the night manager ushered everyone out.

'I want to stay,' his wife begged.

'Of course. Come and sit here and hold his hand.' Rachael
sat the woman where her husband could see her but where
she was out of the way. 'What's his name?'

'Alwyn.'

'And you are?' While Rachael spoke, she continued to
loosen Alwyn's clothing. Joe was checking his mouth, making
sure there was no food or anything blocking the windpipe
before taking a closer look at the pupils.

'Ethel.'

'I'm Rachael and this is Joe.'

'Pulse is weak,' Joe muttered. 'Skin is clammy. Ethel, does
your husband have any allergies or heart problems we should
know about?'

'He takes Lopresor.'

'What does he take that for?'

'An irregular heartbeat.'

'Has he had a check-up recently?' Rachael asked.

'No. I've been telling him to go to the doctor but—'

'What was he doing before the pain struck?' Joe asked as Rachael took the man's pulse.

'He was eating and then he just…he just clutched his chest and started shaking.' Ethel began to cry again.

'Pulse is gone!' Rachael's words were sharp. Joe immediately began mouth-to-mouth resuscitation and Rachael began cardiac heart massage. They were both aware of Ethel's sobs and when the night manager brought the medical kit to them, but their concentration was on getting Alwyn to breathe once more.

Rachael was counting out loud as they worked together. When Alwyn gave a spluttering gasp, she quickly reached for the medical kit, hauled it open and pulled out a stethoscope, handing it to Joe. With a medical torch, she checked his pupils.

'Equal and reacting to light. Stay with us, Alwyn,' she said encouragingly, watching him closely.

'Check out what's in that kit, Rach. Any adrenaline?'

She had a quick check. 'No.'

He shook his head. 'Guess it was a long shot.'

Alwyn was still spluttering and turning a lovely shade of green. Rachael dug around in the medical kit and found a lined bag. Moments later, he vomited. Rachael soothed him as Joe pumped up the portable sphygmomanometer he'd found in the kit.

'Ethel,' Joe said as he worked, 'Alywn's still not out of the woods. It appears he's had a heart attack and will need to be hospitalised. While we're waiting for the ambulance, did you want to call someone to come and be with you?'

'I'll get you a phone,' the night manager said from the doorway, and quickly hurried away.

'My daughter. I'll call her. She'll know what to do.'

'Good.'

'Is he going to be all right?' Ethel's grip on her husband's hand was almost vice-like, and Rachael didn't blame her.

'We can't answer that,' she said softly. 'Once we have him at the hospital and he's had further tests, we'll know more. I can tell you that the next twenty-four hours are critical.'

'BP is still low.'

'Skin's still clammy.' Rachael checked Alywn's pupils again as Joe deflated the sphygmo cuff and reached for the stethoscope. 'Stay with us, Alwyn. We can't do this by ourselves, we need your help. Pupils still equal and reacting.' She pressed her fingers to his pulse. 'Pulse is stronger than before. That's it, Alwyn. Just stay focused on what you need to do.'

'Heart rate is improving. No, Alwyn, don't close your eyes. Just keep looking at Rachael…which isn't hard to do. You've got a beautiful woman on either side of you—lucky man.' At Joe's words, a faint smile touched Alwyn's lips and Rachael saw him squeeze Ethel's hand.

'That's it, love,' his wife encouraged him, brushing the tears from her eyes with her free hand. 'The ambulance is coming and they'll get you to hospital.'

'How's the pain, Alwyn? Is it going away?' Rachael asked. 'Squeeze Ethel's hand again if it's getting better.' Rachael watched the muscles in his hands clench around his wife's small, frail fingers.

'He squeezed.' Ethel was exuberant.

'Good. Just stay nice and calm.'

The night manager came back with a phone, which he handed to Ethel, and the news that the ambulance had just pulled up. He disappeared as quickly as he'd come but returned a minute later with the paramedics.

'Hey, Joe.'

'Smitty. Come and meet Alwyn and Ethel. Alwyn.' Joe turned his attention to their patient. 'This is my friend Smitty and he's going to take great care of you.'

Smitty placed a non-rebreather mask over Alwyn's mouth and nose to administer oxygen.

'We'll have you feeling better in next to no time, mate,' Smitty said with a smile. He glanced from the patient to Rachael. 'Mick Schmidt.' He held his hand out to her.

'Rachael Cusack.'

'It is a *pleasure* to meet you, Rachael.'

'Focus, people,' Joe growled, which only made Rachael smile. She'd heard him use that tone in the past and it had been when another man had attempted to chat her up. 'Smitty, get him ready to transfer to the stretcher.'

While they worked, Ethel finished her call to her daughter and went back to holding her husband's hand. The love they shared for each other was clearly evident in their gazes. Rachael sighed, hoping, longing and wishing that she, too, could have had that long-lasting love. She sneaked a glance at Joe and looked quickly away when she realised he was watching her, a scowl on his face.

When Alwyn was ready, Smitty and his colleague wheeled the stretcher out to the ambulance parked at the front of the hotel. A small crowd had gathered around, curious to see what was going on.

'I'll go with him to the hospital,' Joe said.

'What about your car?'

'I'll come and get it later.' He stood beside the open ambulance doors and looked down at her. 'We'll finish our discussion tomorrow.'

She nodded. 'I don't think you got the answers you were looking for, Joe, but the ones I gave you were honest. I hope you know that.'

'You've never lied to me, Rachael. I respect that.' His voice was as smooth as silk, his gaze a gentle caress. She found it hard not to sigh with longing and held herself aloof.

'Mum!' A car had pulled up behind them and Rachael quickly turned to face her son. 'Mum?' Declan's eyes were wide with panic.

'I'm all right, darling. I'm all right.' She held out her arms and he quickly hugged her. 'A guest had a heart attack and they called me down to help. That's all.'

Declan nodded. 'Dad!' His blue eyes were now wide with surprise.

'Dad?' Smitty said as he stepped from the back of the ambulance, glancing at Joe in surprise. 'Now the growl makes sense.'

Joe ignored the paramedic and turned to face his son.

'Dad, what are you doing here?'

Dad! Joe couldn't believe the swell of pride that washed over him at having that one word directed at him. 'Uh...I just dropped by.'

'Joe,' Smitty said. 'We're ready to go.'

'OK.' He went to climb into the back of the ambulance.

'Let me know how Alwyn gets on,' Rachael said.

Joe nodded. He glanced at Declan and opened his mouth to speak, but Smitty started the engine and the other paramedic was waiting to close the rear doors. Joe looked at Rachael. 'I'll see you tomorrow.'

The doors were shut and the ambulance drove off with flashing lights and blaring sirens.

'Excitement just seems to follow you around,' Rachael's mother said as she came to stand by her daughter and grandson. 'Your father's just going to park the car and will meet us up in your room,' Elizabeth Cusack said, rubbing her hands up and down her arms. 'It's getting chilly out here.'

Until her mother had mentioned it, Rachael hadn't noticed. With Declan's arm still protectively around her shoulders, they headed inside, the night manager thanking her profusely for her help and saying that her night's account would be taken care of.

When they got back to their room, Declan headed off to have a shower and Rachael went to the mini-bar.

'Need a drink?' Elizabeth asked. 'I'm not surprised. I gather that was Joe?'

'Yes.'

'Hmm. I can see why you fell for him.'

'Mum!' Rachael whirled around and looked at her mother in astonishment.

'What? All I'm saying is he's a good-looking man. He has that…rebel-without-a-cause look to him.'

'Yes. He had it in abundance fifteen years ago, too.' Rachael shut the fridge door and slumped down into a chair. 'Oh, Mum. I don't know what to do.'

'Meaning?'

'Meaning I'm still attracted to the man.'

'Of course you are. It's a natural reaction, especially as you weren't the one to end things. The question is, how does Joe feel?'

'I guess he's attracted to me.' She glanced up at her mother. 'We almost kissed.' The instant the words were out of her mouth, she buried her face in her hands. 'Oh-h,' she wailed. 'What am I going to do? I'm so confused.'

'Look.' Elizabeth came over and placed a hand on her daughter's shoulder. 'When you came home from America, we knew something was wrong the instant you stepped off the plane. By the time we'd driven home, we both knew the trouble was a man. We didn't push you because we just thought it was some holiday romance.'

'And then I was pregnant.'

'Yes. Well, we were stunned, but that was nothing compared to you telling us you'd *married* the man, only to have your marriage annulled two days later.' Elizabeth shook her head. 'It just wasn't like you at all. You'd always been firm in your goals, dependable and trustworthy. Not that marrying Joe didn't make you less those things, it was just so…out of character for you.'

'I know.'

'The thing is, darling, if Joe hadn't insisted on the annulment, do you honestly believe the marriage would have lasted?'

'I would have worked at it.'

'I'm not saying you wouldn't have. You would have worked hard, made bigger sacrifices and probably compromised your goals and ambitions to fit in with a life you hadn't planned, but surely you can see that it wouldn't have stood the test of time. Both of you, and I say this only from the things you've told me about Joe over the years, needed to grow up. It's sad he didn't know about Declan but you've both been able to achieve a lot in the past fifteen years. Now he's back in your life and the emotions have swamped you all over again.'

'They're just so…so…*big*. And there's so many of them.'

Elizabeth laughed. 'You'll work it out, darling. You always do. We're here to help you as we've always been. We trust you, Rachael, and we trust your instincts. You'll do what's right. And if that's letting Joe into Declan's life?'

'Then that's what will happen.'

'But what about letting Joe back into *your* life?'

'I don't know,' Rachael wailed.

'How does Declan feel about Joe?'

'How many times did he mention Joe this evening?'

'Quite a few,' Elizabeth confessed.

'Then you hardly need to ask. Now that Joe's appeared out of the blue, Declan's eager to get to know him, and I can't say I blame him. I mean, he's almost fifteen. He's coming to that time in his life when I can't do much except just be there for him. I know he has Dad and it's wonderful that he's had a male influence throughout his life but…'

'This is his father, not his grandfather. I understand.' Elizabeth pulled her chair closer. 'And Joe? Does he want to get to know Declan?'

'I'm not sure. I'm pressuring him.'

'Is that wise?'

'Probably not. I just don't want Declan hurt. Joe either chooses to be part of his son's life or he doesn't. I won't have Declan stressed out about Joe. Not now. He's just got into this school and the last thing he needs is more stress.'

'He's much better at managing his anxiety now, and he's a bright boy.'

'And that concerns me more. It's because he's so smart that he might pick up on things an ordinary teenage boy would overlook. He's so sensitive.'

'There comes a time when you need to trust Declan to make his own decisions. He may decide that two weeks getting to know his father is all he wants, or all he needs for that matter.'

'I doubt that. Joe is…' Rachael shook her head and smiled absently. 'Joe is…encompassing. He can make you feel alive in a way you'd never thought possible. I don't know how he does it but he sort of taps into your inner soul and helps you to feel free.'

'Sounds amazing.'

'He is.'

'I think you need to let Declan and Joe work it out for themselves. Just promise me one thing, darling.'

'What?'

'That you'll try to live in the present. Don't rehash the past over and over. It's easy to get caught in the cycle but there's still an attraction between you and Joe. Remember to look forwards, not backwards.'

Rachael thought about her mother's words long into the night. When Joe had almost kissed her she'd felt as exhilarated as she had all those years ago. He'd always made her feel…wonderful, special and cherished, and for a brief moment tonight those feelings had been there again.

A spark of hope ignited deep inside her and, clinging to it, she finally drifted off to sleep.

*   *   *

Rachael looked at her list of patients. Five more to go and her second day at Joe's practice was done. Only eight more days and she was finished. She'd dressed in a pair of black trousers, flat-heeled shoes and a casual red knit top. If Joe didn't wear a suit to work, she'd decided that she didn't need to wear one either. Comfortable, professional. That was her wardrobe anyway, but it was nice not to have to worry about a certain level of clothing formality as she'd had to at her previous practice.

So far today she'd seen three pregnant women and several children, two of whom had required immunisations. She'd called the hospital that morning and had spoken to Ethel who told her Alwyn's condition was improving.

'His cardiac specialist is quite impressed with his recovery so far, but said he'll know better tomorrow morning.'

'That's great news. Do you mind if I call tomorrow for another update?'

'You don't need to ask, dear. If it wasn't for you and Dr Silvermark…well, I don't even want to think about it.'

'We were just doing our job.'

'Well, I'm grateful, deary. You take care of him now. He's quite a catch and it's quite clear you have eyes only for each other.'

It was? 'I'll speak to you tomorrow,' Rachael replied, and rang off. Was it clear? Could complete strangers see the attraction she and Joe felt for each other? She hadn't seen him all day and part of her felt slightly bereft while the other part knew it was for the best to keep her distance.

Rachael read through the file on her next patient—a little boy who'd seen Alison a few times about tummy pains. He'd been tried on liquid paraffin to help bowel motions, but the pains were still continuing. Alison had already had a white-cell count done to check for appendicitis, but the tummy pain was generally on the left rather than the right side. Alison had also noted little Anthony Edmunds was a tantrum-thrower and, if he wasn't watched could end up with a hernia. Rachael stood and went to call him through. 'Anthony.'

The little boy looked at her and then buried himself in his mother's lap. 'No.'

Rachael went over. 'Hello, Anthony. I'm Dr Rachael. How old are you?' She sat down beside his mother.

'He's almost four.'

'Wow. You're so big.' When she received no response from him, she glanced at his mother. 'What can I do for you today?'

'Out here?' His mother looked around. Rachael followed her gaze. There were only two other people in the waiting room, and as they were both above the age of ten and had no children in tow, she deduced they were Joe's patients. She guessed he was here after all.

'To start with.'

'He keeps saying his tummy's sore. I brought him to see Alison two weeks ago but things aren't getting better.'

'OK.' Rachael turned her attention to her small patient. 'Anthony, did you see this book?' Rachael pulled the book off the small table. 'It's a story about a funny puppy. Do you like puppies?'

The little boy looked over his shoulder. 'No.'

'Oh.' She appeared disappointed. 'I guess you won't like this story, then. I'll just read it to myself.' Rachael opened the book and began to read out loud, holding it in such a way that Anthony could just see the pictures. Regardless of the other patients in the room and the fact that Helen was watching her closely, Rachael kept reading and slowly Anthony edged over, listening intently to what she was saying. By the end of the story he was actually leaning his elbow on Rachael's leg, pointing to the pictures.

'That was fun. Would you like to choose another story?' Without a word he quickly reached for a book about cars. 'Ah, so you're a car man. You're just like my son.' Being careful not to let him know he'd come out of his mood, she held out her hand. 'Come and sit on my knee and we'll read it together.'

Anthony clambered up onto her knee and sat enthralled as she read the story. She was pleased when he joined in with the *brm-brm* sounds she was making. 'You're good at that.' When they'd finished that book, she asked Anthony to choose another one. He did and held it out to her. 'Let's go and read this one somewhere else.' She held out her hand for the little boy to take.

'What a good idea,' his mother said, and stood.

Anthony hesitated for a fraction of a second before slipping his hand into hers, holding his other hand out for his mother. It was then Rachael realised she'd really had an audience while she'd been focused on Anthony. Both of Joe's patients were still sitting in the waiting room and Joe was leaning casually against the reception desk where Helen was beaming brightly at her.

'Good work,' Joe said softly as they passed him. Rachael felt pride sweep over her at his praise. Why could he still do that to her? It wasn't fair that he should be able to affect her so easily.

Rachael continued with the consultation and after sitting Anthony up on the examination bed and reading the next story to him, she was finally able to get him to lie down so she could check his stomach.

'Has he been going to the toilet regularly?'

'Yes.'

'Bowel motions?'

'He's still having a little trouble.'

Rachael could feel that for herself. Anthony's bowels were quite tight.

'How's his appetite?'

'He hasn't been eating as much as he usually does.'

'And the liquid paraffin? Has that been helping?'

'Alison only said to give it to him when he hadn't had bowel motions for three days. He had one yesterday.'

'It can't have been a big one.' Anthony was still looking at the pictures in the book she'd just read him. Gently, she probed his tummy once more. 'Does this hurt, Anthony?'

'Nope.'

'How about here?' She gradually made her way from the right side to the left.

'Nope.'

'Here?' She pressed and he winced in pain.

'Ow. That weally hurts.' His lower lip came out and Rachael immediately smiled at him.

'Thank you for telling me. What a brave boy you are. Would you like to sit up now?' She helped him up. 'Did you see those great toys over there?'

'I played with them last time.'

'Do you want to play with them again?' She helped him down from the examination table as she spoke. Once he was settled, she gestured that his mother should have a seat.

'Has he been crying more or having tantrums?'

'No more than usual,' his mother answered.

'How many tantrums would you say he has a week?'

'Two.' His mother shrugged. 'He's just like other boys his age.'

Rachael smiled, noting the defensive tone. 'You're right, but in Anthony's case those upsets are affecting his bowels. What about diet? Does he eat a lot of fibre? Fruit, breads, cereals?'

'He doesn't like them. I've tried several different types of cereals but he just doesn't like them. He'll eat sandwiches and I buy the white bread which is supposed to be high in fibre.'

'Good. Fruit or vegetables?'

'No. I've tried everything to get him to eat them but he just doesn't like them.'

'What type of foods does he like?'

'Junk food. He'll eat chips—as in French fries—and, as I've said, sandwiches.'

'Biscuits? You can buy biscuits with wheat in them.'

'Tried that. He doesn't like them.'

'Prunes? Dried fruits?'

'No.'

Rachael wrote some notes. 'What about a fever? Has he been overly hot or had a temperature? Chills?'

'He was very hot last night, that's why I had to bring him back in today.'

'Did you take his temperature?'

'He wouldn't hold the thermometer under his tongue.'

'OK.' Rachael reached for her timpani thermometer and walked over to Anthony. 'I'm just going to put this into your ear.'

'Does it tickle?' he wanted to know, and by the time he'd asked the question, the thermometer had beeped, giving Rachael the readout. 'Hey, dat didn't hurt.'

'No, it didn't. That's because you're a big, brave boy.' She returned to her desk. 'It's just a bit above normal. Did you give him anything to bring the temperature down?'

'Just paracetamol.'

'Good. I've read in Anthony's notes that Alison has done some tests. I'd like to do a few more.'

'Such as?'

Rachael smiled apologetically. 'Nothing he's going to like, I'm afraid. I noticed Alison did a stool sample about a month and a half ago. I'd like another one done, as well as a urine test.'

'What do you think it might be?'

'Alison's ruled out appendicitis but because Anthony's still having trouble it's definitely something to do with his bowels. That could be diverticulosis, diverticulitis or he could be on his way to a hernia. The tantrums he's having may be causing the bowel to twist, but then again he could be having the tantrums because that's the only way he knows to effectively communicate that he's in a lot of pain. The other test I'd like him to have is a barium enema.'

'That doesn't sound good.'

'It's not. It's where they put a liquid paste into the rectum and lower colon so when they X-ray the stomach, the information is more accurate.'

'Won't it hurt him?'

'He'll be given a sedative as they also need him to be still while the X-ray is being performed.'

Rachael watched the look of astonishment on the mother's face. 'I can call Dr Silvermark in if you'd like a second opinion.'

'Yes, please.'

'Good.' Rachael checked which number she was supposed to call to get Joe's consulting room, and in another moment he picked up the phone. 'Joe, have you got a minute? I need a second opinion.'

'On the little boy?'

'Yes.'

'Give me two minutes.'

Rachael hung up the phone. 'He'll be here in a moment.'

'You're not angry?'

'About what?'

'About me questioning you…wanting another opinion.'

'No. Not only would that be highly unprofessional of me, it's also quite natural. I'm new here and I'm not giving you news you're comfortable with, so naturally you'd want my opinion confirmed.' Rachael smiled. 'Besides, if it were my son, I'd be wanting a second opinion. Bowels are a sensitive area and so many things can go wrong, but if caught early we can do something about it. By you bringing Anthony in now, I'm pretty sure he's going to be fine.'

Joe knocked on her door and came in. Anthony was just as hesitant to have another person touching his stomach, and after Joe was finished he began to cry. 'It feels as though there's a little bump on the left and it's very tender,' he said. 'I'm not sure what tests Alison has already done but I'd want a blood test, stool and urine samples and X-ray.' Joe added, 'How does that compare with your diagnosis, Dr Cusack?'

'You're spot on,' Anthony's mother said as she cradled her son. 'Thank you.'

'OK.' Joe smiled. 'I'll leave you in Dr Cusack's capable hands, then.' He excused himself and left the room.

'That man has a potent smile,' she muttered to Rachael. 'I've never really had much to do with him before but my husband's seen him and is quite confident about him.'

'Are you happy for me to go ahead and organise the tests?'

'Yes.' Anthony had started to settle down again and Rachael printed off the necessary pathology and X-ray request forms, explaining the procedure to his mother.

'Come and see me next week when we should have all the test results back and we can go from there.'

'In the meantime?'

'You need to get more fibre into him.' She pulled open a cupboard that contained pamphlets on a multitude of topics and handed over the one on dietary fibre. 'This contains a list of foods high in fibre and also ways to prepare them so children will eat them. Also, put him back on the liquid paraffin.' Rachael wrote down the dosages Anthony's mother was to follow for the next week. 'If you have any questions, don't hesitate to call.'

'Thank you.'

Anthony didn't want to leave but was pacified by Rachael promising to read him a story the next time he came and the lolly she gave him for being such a good boy.

Once they were gone, Rachael went to the kitchen for a much-needed cup of coffee.

'You were brilliant with him,' Joe said as he walked in. Rachael stirred her coffee and took a quick sip, hoping it would give her strength. She certainly needed all she could get when she was around Joe. Today he was dressed in a pair of black jeans and a black T-shirt with a chambray shirt hanging open like a jacket. Why did he have to look so good? She pushed her frustrated libido away, deciding her best course of action was to hightail it out of there.

'Thanks.' She washed the spoon and picked up her coffee. 'I'd better get back to it.'

'Hey, listen, Rach.' He put out a hand to stop her and she quickly moved away, almost spilling her coffee. 'Uh…is Declan coming here after school again today?'

'Yes.'

'When's that?'

She checked her watch. 'In about fifteen minutes. Why?'

'Well…I…er…thought I might take him with me to the studio this afternoon.'

'Weren't you there this morning?'

'Yes, but they have an afternoon shoot—call-back.'

'Call-back?'

'A stunt they did the other day didn't go as planned, so they're taking another crack at it.'

'What sort of movie is it?'

'Action sci-fi.'

'Hmm.' She sipped her drink. 'And you want to take Declan.'

'Yes. I just wanted to clear it with you first. I could show him around, he could see a different side to medicine rather than just clinics and hospitals.'

Rachael knew his words were just a cover. It was Joe's way of saying he wanted to spend time with his son. Why he didn't come right out and say it she wasn't sure, but things weren't always straightforward where Joe was concerned.

'OK, but not for too long.'

'Sure. Tell me what time you want him back at the hotel and I'll drop him off.'

'Actually, I'll come to you and pick him up.'

'Right. Good. I'll clear it with the security guard for you.'

'I'd appreciate it. I'll come once I've finished here.'

'That doesn't give us long.'

'How long do you want, Joe?' she asked pointedly.

'I can't answer that just yet.' He held up his hand when she opened her mouth. 'Don't pressure me, Rach. You'll get your answer, but at least let me spend a bit of one-on-one time with him.'

'How about dinner, then? The three of us?'

He hesitated and Rachael bit her lip. Had she pushed him too far…again? 'If you have other plans, we understand. We're hardly here to cramp your romantic style.'

'What?' He frowned. 'Romantic style?' A slow smile spread across his mouth as he realised she was not so subtly fishing. 'I'm not dating anyone, if that's what you're trying to get at.'

'Well, I should hope not, especially after you almost kissed me last night.'

'Hmm.' The smile deepened and he took a step towards her. She stood her ground but held her coffee cup between them. 'Now that I know you're not married, do you want to pick up where we left off?'

'Do you mean from last night or from fifteen years ago, Joe? Because my life has changed considerably in fifteen years and I'm no longer so naïve that I'll fall for the smooth lines you dish out.'

The uncomfortable twitch of his left eye was the only outward sign that she'd riled him. *'Touché.'* He stepped back. 'In that case, I'll leave you to your work and I'll see you later.'

Rachael sat at her desk a little later and shook her head. She was going to have to figure out how to deal with the way Joe made her feel. If he decided he wanted to be a part of Declan's life, she would be seeing quite a bit of him from now on. How would she cope if some other woman did come into his life—a new stepmother for Declan?

'Whoa!' She cut her thoughts off like a stylus sliding along a vinyl record. She stood up and paced her office. 'Don't go there. Declan will be fine. He's a smart boy, well adjusted. Joe's only taking him to a studio where everything is perfectly safe and he'll be fine. You'll pick him up, the three of you will have dinner and then Joe will tell you his decision. It's OK. Everything is OK.'

She did some deep breathing and almost jumped out of her skin when there was a knock at the door. She called for who-ever it was to come in.

'Hi, Mum.' Declan peered around the door.

'It's OK. I don't have a patient here.' He came further into the room and kissed her. 'You're earlier today.'

He shrugged. 'The teacher let us out early.'

'Good. Good. Uh…honey, Joe wants to take you out.'

'Really? He does?'

She tried not to get too concerned about the look of dis-believing pleasure on her son's face. 'Sure, then I'll come and pick you up and the three of us will have dinner.' It did occur to her that Joe hadn't actually agreed to dinner, but tough luck. He was lumbered with the two of them whether he liked it or not.

'Awesome. Can I leave my bag here?'

'Of course. I'll bring it later.'

'You're the greatest, Mum. I'm going to tell Helen.' And with that, he rushed off.

Once more Rachael forced herself to remain under control. It was all right. Declan had gone out with other people plenty of times. He'd gone to lots of different places with his friends back in Cairns. He'd gone out with her parents and had spent time away from her on school camps, so why was she so worried about a few hours with his father?

The answer came hard on the question's heels. Because Joe had the power to hurt him.

Rachael continued to go through the calming exercises she'd been using for years and finally called her next patient through. The sooner she finished here, the sooner she could head out to the studio to see exactly what it was Joe did when he wasn't here.

Her last few patients seemed to want to chat and she finished over an hour later than she was supposed to. She took the patient files out to Helen and was thankful when the other woman didn't keep her talking.

'Go and see how the boys are getting on.'

'Try and stop me,' she muttered, heading out to her car. She followed the directions to the studio Helen had handed her, and was pleased to find there was no problem about her wandering around in the area roped off to tourists. The theme park was a place she wanted to return to, but for now she had other matters on her mind…namely finding her son.

'Excuse me,' she said, stopping a man who wore an official-looking badge on a chain around his neck. 'I'm looking for Joe Silvermark.'

'Ah, Joe. Joe's through here.' The man led her into a large hangar. To Rachael's surprise it contained several sets and equipment.

'Have you finished for the day?'

'We've nailed one scene but the major stunt is after dinner. Mind the cables.' He took her through the building. 'Have you known Joe long?'

'Well…' She glanced at his badge again. 'Er…Wong, it's a long story.'

'You the boy's mother?' Wong nodded, answering his own question. 'Of course. You're very beautiful. I can see why Joe likes you and why he needed to pound his frustrations out on the punching bag.' Wong chuckled to himself. 'They're out here.' They continued to the other side of the hangar and came out the other end. 'Over there.'

Wong pointed to a large crane set up on the back lot. Rachael's eyes took a moment to adjust to being back out in the daylight. 'They'll be down in a minute.' Wong smiled at his own joke, and as he spoke she saw a person jump off the crane.

Her heart leapt into her throat before she realised the person was bungee jumping. Down—then back up, and then down again. It was then she realised Joe was the person doing the human yo-yo impersonation.

'Oh, my gosh. I can't believe he just did that.' She placed her hand on her chest, surprised to find it pounding hard.

'Joe? He's done it thousands of times. He's just trying to give the boy confidence.'

'*Boy?* What *boy*?' Rachael squinted as she peered up to the top of the crane. There was a small platform there, and to her complete horror she realised the figure standing up there, waiting to jump, was her son.

'Declan!' His name came out in a terrified whisper.

CHAPTER FOUR

'JOSEPH MITCHELL SILVERMARK!'

Rachael had waited while Joe had been hoisted back up to the top and had had his bungee cord removed. As Joe had climbed back down the ladder, the anger in her was ready to burst. She stormed over to her ex-husband.

'Rach! You're earlier than we expected.' If it was possible for him to blanch, she was sure he did.

'You get him down from there this instant.'

'He's all right, Rach. He *wants* to do it.'

'He suffers from anxiety and stress, Joe. Didn't I tell you that? He might be freaking out right now and—'

'If he changes his mind, it's fine. He can come down the normal way.'

'I can't believe you've done this. You've been with him for a few hours and you're already putting him in danger.'

'Rachael—'

'No, Joe. Don't you "Rachael" me. If he ends up with nightmares tonight, *I'm* the one who'll be looking after him.'

'Nightmares? Rachael, he's almost fifteen.'

'And that just shows how much you know about him. You don't think ahead, Joe. You just go with whatever whim you—'

'Ready,' a bloke called out and Rachael was paralysed to the spot as she heard a cry.

'Three, two, one, *bungee!*'

'I think I'm going to be sick,' she muttered, and felt her knees weaken. Joe's arm came about her shoulders and she leaned into him, not wanting to watch but unable to take her eyes off her son for an instant. Declan hesitated and then jumped off—flying down towards them with his arms out wide.

She was positive the rope wasn't going to stop him. Positive he was going to hit the ground with a thud and break every bone in his body—at the least.

But just as had happened with Joe, the rope caught him like a giant spring and sent him back up again. She didn't even want to contemplate the damage that might be done to his spine, being jerked around like that.

'He's fine, Rach. Breathe. Breathe.' Joe's words penetrated her head and she belatedly sucked air into her lungs. 'See. He's fine.' Joe squeezed her shoulder before running over to where Declan's bounce was practically at an end.

Rachael watched as her son was hoisted back to the top before he was unhooked. Joe had climbed the steps once more to be there for his son. She watched as Declan wrapped his arms around Joe and the almost hesitant way Joe put his arms around his son for the first time.

A lump formed in her throat and she closed her eyes against the tears that were threatening to overflow. When she opened them it was to find them both climbing down the steps, and when her son's feet were safely back on terra firma, Rachael let out a deep sigh.

Declan rushed over and threw his arms about her shoulders. 'Mum! Mum! Wasn't that amazing?' His face was alive with an exuberant delight Rachael had never seen before. He couldn't stand still and reminded her of when he'd been a little boy and had desperately needed to go to the toilet. 'Wow! I can't believe I just did that.' He let out a loud whoop which made her jump. 'So cool.' He turned to face his father. 'That was the best. You were right, Joe. How cool!'

Joe looked at Rachael. 'See? He's fine.'

But are you? Rachael wanted to ask him. She could see a hint of stunned bewilderment in Joe's gaze at the way Declan had embraced him. Would he ever get used to the affectionate ways of their son? She certainly hoped so because if he didn't, it could destroy Declan.

'What's next?' Declan asked, and Joe laughed.

'That's it for tonight, mate. I think your mother's had enough surprises over the last forty-eight hours.' He leaned closer to Declan and said in a lower voice, 'And I'm trying to get back into her good books.'

'Really?' Rachael knew she was supposed to hear the comment and could see the teasing glint in Joe's blue eyes. 'Why would you want to do that, Joe?'

'Ah, trade secret. Right now, though…' he rubbed his hands together in delight '…it's time for dinner. Unfortunately, I need to stay close to the studio as we haven't finished and will probably be going for a few more hours, but if you don't mind eating with the rest of the cast and crew, there's a great feast put on just over there.' He pointed towards another large hangar.

'Cool. Are the actors going to be there?'

Joe nodded.

Declan looked at his mother. 'Can we? *Please?* Joe told me who the lead actor is, and he's the same guy from the movie we watched last night, Mum. And he's just through there.' Declan pointed to the hangar. 'Can we, Mum? *Please?* I promise I'll do my homework the instant we get back to the hotel. *Please?*'

It had been so many years since Declan had pleaded for anything that Rachael was inclined to give in right there and then. She looked at Joe and then back at her son. Both were wearing identical expressions, just like small children who really wanted to open their Christmas presents early. She couldn't help it and burst out laughing, feeling the tension of the past few days ease out of her.

'Does that mean yes?' Declan asked.

'All right, but so long as we're not intruding?'

'Yes!' Declan pumped the air with his fist before leaning over to kiss her cheek. 'You're the greatest.'

Joe leaned over and kissed her other cheek. 'You *are* the greatest.' He looked at his son. 'Let's go eat.'

Declan linked his arm through his mother's on one side and Joe followed suit on the other. Between the two of them, she was almost propelled into the room where there seemed to be hundreds of people sitting at tables, eating and laughing. The noise was so loud she thought she'd need earplugs. Joe found them a table and then took Declan over to meet the lead actors. Rachael watched Joe, his chest puffed out proudly as he introduced his son. She actually saw the words 'my son' form on Joe's lips and sighed with relief. Joe had accepted Declan.

He motioned for her to come over but she felt too self-conscious and shook her head. She liked watching the two of them together and was still astounded at the similarities. Joe had been nineteen when they'd met, and that's how old Declan would be in just over four years' time. They had the same physique, although Declan was still a miniature version, his shoulders not as broad, his height less…but she knew he'd get there. She'd known from the instant she'd first held her son that he was going to be as devastatingly handsome as his father.

Rachael closed her eyes, praying she'd done the right thing by letting Declan get to know Joe. Would Joe hurt him the way he'd hurt her? She had no idea but, whatever happened, both she and Declan would work it out…somehow.

She opened her eyes and discovered they'd gone. She quickly scanned the room and found them at the large buffet, loading food onto their plates, both of them laughing. When had Declan last been this animated? She couldn't remember. For the past few years since he'd started high school, he'd been very serious, very dedicated to his work and sometimes pushing himself way too hard. Sure, they'd joked and laughed but not like this.

They headed over, both carrying trays loaded with food.

'Here's one for you,' Declan said, handing her a plate. 'I wasn't sure whether you liked prawns but Joe told me you did.'

'Well, she *used* to.' His gaze met Rachael's and she felt her heart rate increase with delighted excitement. He was looking at her as though he'd just won the lottery and didn't have a clue what to do with the winnings. Was that look for her? Was it because of Declan? Either way, it was creating havoc with her equilibrium. The smile on his lips was small yet intimate—she remembered it well.

'He's right. I do like them.'

'Oh. Can I try one?'

'Sure.' Rachael was pleasantly surprised that her son was willing to try a new food.

'But if you like it, you can get your own,' Joe added, pinching one off Rachael's plate and showing him how to shell the prawn.

'Delicious. We should have these at least once a week, Mum.' Declan was out of his chair and heading to the buffet again.

Rachael laughed in astonishment. 'Once a week. Oh, sure, son,' she said to his retreating back.

Joe joined in her laughter. 'I guess he doesn't have any idea how much they cost.'

'So?'

'So, what?'

'Joe. You've obviously decided you want to get to know Declan better, but for how long?'

He shrugged. 'I don't know, Rach. He's a great kid.'

'No argument there, and you've only spent a few hours with him.'

Joe stole another prawn off her plate.

'Hey! Get your own.' She slapped playfully at his hand but he was too quick for her. 'I will say that Declan has many moods.' She grinned at him. 'Just like his father.' Joe merely raised his eyebrows and continued peeling the prawn. 'I think it's wise for you to spend time with him but I reiterate what I said yesterday—I won't have him hurt.'

'I agree with you.' He ate the seafood and wiped his fingers on a napkin. 'I hardly slept last night.'

'Join the club.' Declan returned with a huge plateful of food. 'Declan!'

'It's all right, Mum. Ivan—he's the cook up there—said I could take whatever I wanted, especially as I was Joe's son. He said that Joe saved his life a few years ago and he thinks he's the best person in the world.'

They both looked at Joe who seemed highly uncomfortable with the praise. He shrugged. 'It's just the job. Ivan used to be a stuntman and he was in a bad accident and... You know the drill, Rach. As doctors, we do what it takes.'

Rachael nodded but wasn't surprised to find such high praise about the man sitting opposite her. 'So you've been doing this movie work for some time now?'

'Five years. It's not full-time, only when there's a movie being shot here, and that's usually once every six months. It also depends on the number of stunts they do. Sometimes we're here, sometimes we're on location.'

'So you share your time between here and the clinic for six months, and the other six months?'

He smiled. 'I'm full-time at the clinic.'

'So for six months you work like a normal person and for the other six months you get to play around on a movie set, eating copious amounts of food.'

Joe grinned. 'Fringe benefits.' He shrugged nonchalantly. 'There's not much to my life at all. No dramas, no excitement. Boring ol' Joe, that's me.'

She laughed, not believing a word he said. 'Your nonchalance gives you away every time, Joe.' It was one of his defensive weapons but she'd broken through it before. When he was doing something nice for someone and he didn't want anyone to know about it, nonchalance was his best friend. Joe didn't think he warranted praise about Ivan and she understood his comment about just doing his job, but sometimes people went above and beyond the call of duty.

Although, she reflected, he hadn't been nonchalant on the day he'd asked for the annulment. That had been how she'd known he'd been serious. At first she'd thought he'd been joking, then defensive, then pushing her away for some reason, but in the end—as he'd stood firm in his convictions—she'd realised he hadn't really wanted her for anything but sex.

Rachael pushed the thought away. Now was definitely not the time. Looking down at her plate, she realised she'd eaten far more than she'd thought and now felt a little queasy. She glanced across at Declan's plate and was surprised to find him almost finished. 'Where do you put it all?' she asked rhetorically, smiling at her son.

'I'm a growing kid, Mum.'

'Don't go overboard on the prawns. I don't want you getting stomachache.'

'Spoken like a true mother,' Declan teased, and they laughed.

A bell rang, startling her.

'What's that?' Declan asked the question on her lips.

'Five more minutes and we're to be back on set.'

'Can we stay?' Again, her son's imploring blue gaze was settled on her.

'Actually, it might be fun to watch,' Joe said. 'We're filming a stunt.'

'Do the actors do them?' Declan asked.

'Sometimes, but not tonight. This one's too dangerous.'

'But not for the stunt team, right?' His boyish eyes were wide with unrepressed excitement.

Joe smiled. 'That's right. Wong—you met him earlier—is the stunt coordinator and he and his team are going to jump a car between two trucks.'

'Sounds dangerous.' Rachael frowned.

'There's an element of danger in all stunts, Rach. Wong

and his team have rehearsed the stunt and calculated everything down to the nth degree.'

'Accidents do happen, though, Joe.'

'Yes, they do, and that's why I'm here. Tonight there will also be the fire brigade and at least one ambulance on set. All precautions are taken and we all know what jobs we need to do.'

'Maybe we'd better not stay.' She watched as Declan's face fell.

'If you think you're going to be in the way, don't. I wouldn't let you stay if I thought that.'

Rachael checked her watch, admitting she was curious as well. Declan once more wore his pleading face. 'OK, but not for long.'

'You're the greatest, Mum.' He smiled at her in that familiar way which she knew would someday have the women melting at his feet—just like his father.

They finished eating and made their way back with the rest of the cast and crew. They headed in the opposite direction from where they had been before, and soon found themselves on a back lot which was a huge piece of tarmac. She was surprised to find how dark it had become while they'd been eating, but the back lot was lit with enormous spotlights, ensuring everyone could see quite clearly what was going on.

Rachael was fascinated as she watched the second unit director and Wong give last-minute instructions to the stunt team. There were people everywhere, manning cameras, rigging explosions, taping down cables, all working together towards one common goal.

Joe took Rachael and Declan over to the medical section and reintroduced them to Smitty and his ambulance colleague.

'A lovely surprise to see you again so soon,' Smitty said to Rachael as he shook her hand, holding it for a fraction of a second longer than was necessary. Joe glared daggers at him.

'Easy, Joe.' Smitty laughed. 'And this is your son, eh? You and Joe?' He raised an interested eyebrow.

'Yes.' Rachael felt no need to explain as it really wasn't any of the paramedic's business.

'The resemblance is as plain as day.'

'That's what everyone says.' Declan smiled proudly.

Rachael turned to Joe. 'So what's going to happen here?'

Joe pointed out to the tarmac where two semitrailers were parked—a small gap between the rear of one and the front of the other. 'We're going to jump a car through the gap between the trucks.'

'Are the trucks going to be moving?' Declan asked.

'No. They will be in the movie but that part's already been shot. This is just the camera angles of the jump between the trucks.'

'There are cameras in there?'

'They have cameras everywhere. When we're doing a stunt like this, sometimes you only get one crack at it. The more cameras they have rolling, covering the different angles, the easier it is for the directors and producers to choose which ones they need.'

'There's a fire truck over there.' Declan pointed to where two men were dressed in full firefighting gear.

'As I said, all safety angles are covered.'

'But plenty of people have suffered severe injuries as well as being killed during stunts,' Rachael pointed out.

'Surprisingly, not as many as you'd think, and nine times out of ten the people who have died while doing stunts either didn't work out the angles correctly or didn't take the necessary safety precautions. Sometimes producers cut corners to meet their budget constraints, which means not enough money to do the stunt properly. Sometimes the stunt people involved aren't as qualified as they make out. Wong knows every single person on his team and knows exactly what they're capable of. He's highly sought-after for a lot of action films, and at the moment I think he's booked solid for the next four years.'

Rachael was surprised. 'What? One movie after another?'

'That's his job, Rach.' She shook her head, quite bemused. 'The actors are booked for longer than that. The guy who's playing the lead in this movie has his shooting schedule worked out for the next six years.'

'Wow! That's amazing.' Rachael and Declan watched this alien world with continued amazement.

Wong headed over to them. 'Joe, you set?'

'All ready. How's it looking?'

'Good. Almost ready to go.' He looked at Rachael. 'There are going to be loud explosions so cover your ears, OK? You, too.' He pointed to Declan. 'Got to take care of Joe's family.'

Rachael smiled at him, deciding to ignore his last remark. 'Thanks for the warning.' Wong headed back and Joe pulled on a headset so he could listen to what was going on.

'Joe? Where are the explosions?' Rachael asked, peering closely at the vehicles.

Joe pointed to the truck in the rear. 'In there. The truck explodes in the movie.'

'Why?'

'Because someone has just shot a missile at the car and that's why the car is jumping between the trucks, and the missile hits the second truck instead.'

'Oh.' Rachael frowned. 'What about the poor truck driver?'

Joe laughed. 'What truck driver?'

'In the movie. What about the truck driver?'

'The truck driver isn't important to the story.'

'But does he get out in time? Is he hurt?'

Joe smiled. 'I don't know, but if it makes you feel any better, I'll raise your concerns with the director and find out.'

'Thank you.' She couldn't help the tingles that spread through her from his smile. It really was lethal.

'Ready on the set.' The call came and Rachael reached for Declan's hand, giving it an excited squeeze. She watched him for a second and again saw animated delight on his face. She was thankful to Joe for giving him this experience...even if it meant Declan would hardly sleep tonight.

'Quiet on the set,' came the next call, and Declan dropped his mother's hand to watch intently. Rachael shifted out of his way and turned to glance at Joe, only to find him watching her. She hadn't realised just how close they were to each other. Joe took a step closer and she could feel the warmth emanating from his body.

His gaze seemed to devour her and she gasped at the intensity she saw in his blue depths. Her heart rate doubled in an instant and a flood of excitement ripped through her. She tried to swallow but found her mouth dry and licked her lips.

He groaned when her tongue flicked out and he embraced the instant tightening in his gut. His gaze flicked to her lips and the need to have them pressed against his was overwhelming. He wasn't used to these sensations any more and she'd been the only woman who had ever made him feel this way. Her lips were still parted in anticipation—he could almost taste her.

'Rach.' The deep timbre of his voice made her tremble in a way she thought she'd never experience again. 'You drive me crazy.'

'Mmm.' She was incapable of forming rational or even irrational sentences. All that mattered was the way Joe made her feel. She was alive—truly alive for the first time in fifteen years. How would he react when he learned there had been no other? That he was her one and only true love? He'd hurt, humiliated and rejected her, yet for some masochistic reason she'd remained in love with him and knew it was a love which would last for ever.

He shifted ever so slightly, coming to stand behind her. No longer holding her gaze, he looked unseeingly out at what was happening on the set. She did the same, not really seeing a thing but instead focusing on the way he made her feel.

She gasped again and bit her lip as their fingers touched. The slight roughness of his skin tingled against her soft hands as he tenderly refamiliarised himself with that one small part of her. His arm brushed against her body, sending shocks of pleasure through her.

He laced his fingers with hers, squeezed her hand and her desire grew. He was touching her. He wanted her. Her eyelids fluttered closed for a fraction of a second as she worked hard to control her outward expression. He shifted closer, his body brushing her shoulder. She couldn't breathe but it didn't seem to matter. All she needed was him, and right now she had him.

'I can't take it.' The words were whispered for only him to hear.

'I know. You drive me insane. You always have.'

'Joe.'

'I need you.'

'I know.'

The director called 'Action' over a loudspeaker which made her jump, her back pressing into Joe's. He dropped her hand to steady her, his enigmatic scent winding itself around her. Both of them kept their gazes locked straight ahead, looking as though they were focusing on what was happening before them while all the time their bodies were conducting a completely different action sequence.

The car revved its engine then a squeal of tyres was heard, the smell of burning rubber filling the air. The stunt driver picked up speed, heading for the ramp that would help tip the car up on two wheels, not only to make it slim enough to fit between the two trucks but to also help get the car airborne.

A loud explosion shocked them both and they sprang apart like guilty teenagers, severing all contact. Joe was there one minute and gone the next, grabbing his emergency medical kit before he left. Rachael scanned the area wildly, trying to figure out what had happened. She turned to see Smitty and his colleague rushing over after Joe.

The scene played out before them in slow motion as she and Declan stood there, completely stunned as people yelled, people ran, everyone doing what they were supposed to be doing in order to fix whatever had gone wrong.

'Mum?' Declan reached for her and she held his hand. 'What happened?'

'I don't know, darling.'

The firefighters were heading towards where the car had now come to rest on its roof a long way off from where Joe had said it should land. She scanned the area for Joe but couldn't find him.

'That car's lost a wheel.' Declan pointed to the stunt car. 'Where's the wheel?'

As Declan spoke, Rachael saw Joe crouch down beside someone and rip open his medical kit.

'Over there.' The food she'd eaten earlier churned in her stomach as she saw the wheel not far from where Joe was bending over his patient. He glanced over to where she and Declan were still standing and motioned for her to come over.

'Joe needs me.' She took a deep breath to calm her stomach, straightened her shoulders and put her professional face on. 'Stay here, Declan.'

'But, Mum…'

She thrust her bag at him. 'Call your grandparents and ask them to come pick you up. I don't know how long I'll be here.'

'Can't I stay and help? I can help someone while I'm waiting, can't I? I can carry things, I can make drinks.'

'I don't know what the protocol is.' It was then she spotted Ivan, who'd served Declan that hefty helping of prawns. 'Excuse me,' she called, and he came over. 'Can you help us?'

'I want to help,' Declan said earnestly.

'I need to get to Joe.'

Ivan looked at the two of them. 'You go,' he said to Rachael. 'Come on, mate. You can help me. I'll take good care of Joe's son, you can be sure of that,' he promised.

Declan handed his mother back her bag. 'You call Grandma and I'll help out till she comes.'

Rachael nodded and quickly made the call, telling her mother to mention Joe's name to the security guard. Then she left her bag at the medical station and headed over to help.

'Declan OK?' Joe asked, as she knelt down beside him and pulled on a pair of gloves.

'He's fine.' Rachael turned her attention to their patient and gasped when she realised Joe's patient was his friend, Wong. 'Status?'

'Unconscious. BP's dropping. Pupils sluggish. Chest sounds tight. Airway's clear. He's bleeding somewhere but I'm not sure where. Check his legs.'

Rachael reached for a pair of heavy-duty scissors from Joe's kit and started cutting away Wong's jeans before beginning her examination. 'Left femur has lacerations, left tib-fib feels fractured. Right is fine.'

'Left femoral artery?'

Rachael took a closer look. 'Doesn't look like it.' Joe was setting up an IV drip as Smitty came over.

'Anything you need?'

'Need to intubate and get him out a.s.a.p.'

'I've called it in. Reinforcements are on their way.' Smitty rifled through Joe's extensively stocked medical kit, handing the equipment to Joe as he needed it.

'Checking abdomen,' Rachael said. She cut away Wong's shirt and both she and Smitty gasped. 'I'd say every rib is broken.'

'Did he get hit by the wheel?' Smitty was astounded as he secured a cervical collar around Wong's neck.

'Yes.' The one word from Joe was clipped yet full of emotion.

'Rino—ah, he's the stunt driver,' Smitty added for Rachael's benefit, 'feels to have fractured both legs. He's conscious, BP is slightly higher but that's to be expected. Collarbone doesn't feel too good either and he's probably got a case of whiplash, but he's had so many I think he's used to it. My partner's just fixing him up now.' Smitty paused for a breath. 'They've checked the car. The axle sheared right off.'

'And that's how the wheel came off?' Rachael asked, as she gently touched Wong's abdomen. 'The bleeding's internal. Smitty, get a bag of plasma going.'

The paramedic headed off and was back with the equipment they needed. He set up the plasma while Joe finished intubating Wong. Rachael took his vital signs again. 'BP still not good. Pupils still sluggish. Stay with us, Wong.'

'Let's get him ready to transfer.' Joe gave the order, firmly in control of the situation. He glanced at Rachael but the look on his face was that of a stranger. She'd received that look from him before—on the day of their annulment—and it was one that still had the ability to freeze her heart.

Her eyes widened in alarm and all the insecurities she'd thought she'd dealt with fifteen years ago came flooding back in that one instant. Why was he looking at her like that? She was here. She was helping. There was no cause for him to treat her this way. Her mind began to search through a list of reasons, the list she'd come up with all those years ago for him treating her the way he had, but at the moment she needed to focus on her job.

She pushed them away and they all went…all except one. The question started repeating itself over and over in her mind. It had refused to be pushed away fifteen years ago and it was refusing to go now.

What had she done wrong?

CHAPTER FIVE

'READY to transfer,' Smitty said.

Rachael found it hard to look at Joe as they did their job. She ripped off her gloves and rolled them up into a ball, glancing around for a bin.

'Over there.' Joe pointed when he realised what she was looking for. 'Smitty, take Wong. I'll get to the hospital as soon as the situation is stabilised here.'

Smitty nodded as he wheeled the patient towards the waiting ambulance. 'What's next?' she asked Joe, as he picked up his medical kit and carried it over to where the stunt driver was lying on the ground not far from the car wreck. They knelt down and pulled on gloves.

'Hi. I'm Rachael,' she said to both the patient and the two men with him. The patient had a blanket over him and when she lifted it, it was to find his shirt had already been cut open. He was wearing shorts and work boots—the costume the real actor would be wearing in the movie, she realised.

'This is Rino,' Joe said. 'What have you broken this time?' He smiled down at his friend as he started to check him out.

'Legs,' Rino said, his eyes still closed. 'How's Wong?'

Rachael knew whenever there was bad news to give, the easiest way was to come right out and say it. 'He's not good.'

Rino clenched his jaw and squeezed his eyes even tighter. 'Should have checked it out more thoroughly. It's my fault.'

'We all should have checked it out more thoroughly,' the other man sitting beside Rino said. 'How were we to know the axle was going to shear? We take every precaution possible, we check and double-check, but still things happen.'

'It's my fault,' Rino said again.

'Nah, mate. It's the manufacturer's fault for not testing the axle properly. There's no way we could have foreseen this happening,' Joe remarked.

Rachael checked Rino's pupils and was pleased to find them equal and reacting to light. She listened to his chest and took his blood pressure, which was slightly elevated—but that was to be expected.

'So you've been in a few accidents?' she remarked, as Joe drew up an injection of pethidine.

He smiled and opened his eyes. 'Yeah. Quite a few. Never had a doc as pretty as you look after me, though. It's nice to have a change from Joe's ugly mug.'

Rachael laughed.

'You're brave, saying such things when I'm holding a needle,' Joe countered.

'Pethidine?' Rachael queried quietly.

'He's allergic to morphine.' He indicated the Medic-Alert chain around Rino's neck and Rachael read it. Joe knew these people and she was glad he'd stayed, even though she knew he'd desperately wanted to go to the hospital to be with Wong.

'This should help until the ambulance arrives,' Joe said. 'Then we'll get you hooked up to an IV and a bag of plasma.'

'I know the drill.' Rino closed his eyes again. 'Every bone has been broken at one time or another.'

'Then I'd say you definitely know the drill.' Rachael and Joe checked his legs. 'Possible fractures to right tibia and fibula. Left doesn't feel as bad, except for the laceration above your knee. Can you wiggle your toes for me?' He could. 'Good. Do your legs feel funny, like they have pins and needles?'

'No. Spine doesn't feel broken.'

'Really?' she raised her eyebrows. 'When was the last time you broke it?'

'Two years ago,' Joe answered for him, a teasing note in

his voice. 'He has volumes one and two in casenotes and X-ray packets at the hospital.'

'Everything's well documented, then,' Rachael commented.

'Good. We'll add a few more X-rays to the packet when we get there.'

'Just to be on the safe side,' Joe added.

Rachael continued checking his ribs. 'Right T4 and 5 don't feel good. Left side is good.' She felt her way to his collarbone. 'Clavicle is fractured on the right side.' She felt both shoulder joints, thankful they didn't feel dislocated. She made her way down his arm but couldn't feel anything. 'Wiggle your fingers for me.' He did. 'Squeeze my fingers.' He did. 'Good.'

The sound of the ambulance sirens could be heard. 'Sounds like your ride,' she told him. 'You have a bruise from the safety harness but thank goodness you were wearing it.'

'I'm safety conscious,' he remarked. 'We all are.'

'Joe told me that earlier.'

'Still didn't help,' Rino growled.

'You and I both know these things happen from time to time and it's no one's fault.'

'But Wong—'

'Wong is receiving the best medical attention, just as you will. Leave it for now.' Joe's words were final as he placed a bandage over the large laceration on Rino's left leg. 'It'll need stitches but this will hold you until you get to Accident and Emergency. Rach, do his obs again.'

As the ambulance arrived, Rachael looked over and saw her parents being directed by a security guard onto the back lot. They looked as lost as she'd felt when she'd first arrived. She glanced around for Declan but couldn't see him.

'I'll go to the next patient,' Joe said, also catching sight of her parents. 'Hand over to the paramedics and get Declan sorted out.'

Rachael nodded and did as he asked. She smiled down at Rino as he was loaded into the ambulance. 'Don't give the paramedics too much of a hard time, even though you know the drill.'

He smiled. 'I'll try not to.'

As the ambulance driver shut the doors, Rachael turned and looked around her, not sure where to go or what to do next. She spotted Declan putting a blanket around someone and headed over.

'How are you holding up?' She put her arm around his waist.

'Yeah, good.' He looked around the lot and gave a satisfied nod. 'I just wish I knew more stuff, then I could help more.' He frowned for a moment before looking at her. 'I want to be a doctor, Mum.'

Rachael's eyes widened in surprise. 'Really?'

'Why so surprised? You're a doctor. Joe's a doctor.' He shrugged in that self-conscious way she recognised so well.

Rachael squeezed him closer. 'That's great, Dec. It's great that you've got a direction…just as long as you're making the decision for the right reasons.'

'I want to help people.'

Rachael nodded seriously. 'OK. We'll check out what the entry requirements are for university and go from there.' She kissed his cheek. 'I'm so proud of you.'

'Mum! Not here.' He shrugged out of her embrace but she wasn't offended. 'Look, Grandma and Grandad are here.'

'I saw.' She looked over to where the security guard was talking to one of the crew. Rachael met her mother's gaze and beckoned them over. The security guard looked hesitant but then the crew member pointed to Declan. The security guard peered at Declan for a moment before nodding knowingly. Rachael smiled.

'I didn't think we'd ever find you,' Elizabeth said, kissing her daughter's cheek. 'Thank goodness Declan looks like Joe, otherwise I'm sure the security guard thought we were trying to gatecrash the film shoot rather than just trying to collect our grandson.'

'Come in handy, do I?' Declan smiled.

'Sounds reasonable,' her father added. 'All right, Declan. Let's get you home.'

'Is my homework in your car, Mum?'

'Yes, but don't worry too much about it tonight, Dec.' Rachael smiled up at him. 'Just try and unwind. OK?'

He shrugged. 'Sure, Mum.'

'Thanks for your help, Dr Declan.' Declan's grin was instantaneous and he even blushed a little.

'I'll just get my bag so I can give you my keys. I'll need to go to the hospital with Joe once we're finished here, so if you can take my car back to your house now, that will help. I'll get Joe to drop me there later.' She also wanted to confront Joe about those looks he'd been giving her.

'When can we expect you?' Elizabeth asked.

'I have no idea. Depends how long things take at the hospital.'

'All right, dear.'

As they left, she looked around for Joe and headed over once she'd spotted him. 'Need any help?' she asked.

'All stable here,' he remarked, not looking up as he finished bandaging a woman's arm. 'Go home and rest,' he told his patient. 'Take paracetamol six-hourly and call me if you have any problems.'

'Are you sure I can't just spend the night in hospital? My husband's going to be watching over me as I sleep. He's such a worry wart.'

Joe laughed. 'It's probably good if you're monitored tonight and I'm sure your husband would do an excellent job, but I'm not expecting any complications from your arm. They're all textbook injuries.'

'Thanks, Joe.'

Just then Ivan came over, his face white. 'Joe. One of the girls has just started twitching and we don't know what's wrong.'

'Where?' Joe had already ripped off his old gloves and repacked his bag. 'Rach.' He nodded to her and, following Ivan, they rushed over, being careful of the cables and debris on the ground. The woman was shaking and twitching around on the ground, the blanket she'd had over her body tangling around her legs. Rachael removed the blanket.

'How long has she been like this?' she asked the people around her as she checked the woman's airway. No one answered. 'How long?' she repeated forcefully.

'O-only a m-minute or so,' someone stammered.

'Call the ambulance. What's her name?'

'Grace,' Joe supplied.

'Right. Loosen her clothing and, Ivan, make sure she doesn't kick anything or hit herself. Don't restrain her completely, just make sure she doesn't do further injury to herself.'

Rachael looked into Joe's bag as he checked Grace's airway.

'Airway's clear.'

'Good. Do you have phenytoin?'

'Yes.'

Rachael found what she needed and drew up an injection. 'Make sure she doesn't swallow her tongue,' she said as Grace's body kept twitching. She administered the drug and almost straightaway Grace stopped convulsing, her muscles still alternating between rigidity and relaxation. She looked at the patient. 'Grace?'

Joe checked her airway again. 'Clear.'

Rachael reached for the medical torch. 'Grace? Can you hear me?'

'Yes...' The word came out squeaky and broken. Grace coughed.

'I'm Rachael. I'm a doctor. I'm just going to check your eyes.' Pupils were equal and reacting to light. 'Good. They're good.' She reached for the stethoscope. 'I'm going to listen to your chest now. Just relax. Can you hear me, Grace?'

'Yes.' The word was stronger this time.

'Good.' Rachael listened to her chest and was pleased to find everything fine. 'Do you know where you are?'

'Back lot at the studio.'

'Good. Cognitive reasoning is clear.'

'Ambulance should be here soon,' someone said over her shoulder.

'What happened?' Grace asked, and Rachael realised the woman was starting to feel self-conscious and embarrassed.

'You had a seizure.' It was Joe who answered, his voice calm yet authoritative. He wrapped the sphygmomanometer cuff around Grace's arm and took her blood pressure. 'What's the ETA on the ambulance? I want minutes, not *soon*,' Joe instructed quietly, and Ivan directed someone to find out. 'We need to get you to hospital, Grace. We don't know why you had a seizure and we need to find out. Have you ever had one before?'

'No.'

'Have you been in an accident recently?'

'No. Not for about three months.'

'That's right. You had that concussion,' Joe said. 'That was when you were in America filming, wasn't it?'

'Yes. Got hit in the head with debris when they were blowing up a building.'

'Right. The price of stunt work. Ever had an EEG? That's where they scan your brain,' he explained.

'Yes. I had one then but everything was all ri—' Grace stopped speaking, her eyes widening as she glanced wildly at Rachael. She gestured for her to come closer.

'What's wrong?' Rachael leaned closer.

'I feel all…wet.' Grace tried to sit up but Rachael stopped her, urging her to stay still.

'If you sit up now, you'll be very dizzy. I'm just going to check your arms and legs. Does it hurt anywhere?'

'No.'

Rachael checked her legs and then realised what Grace had meant by 'wet'. She reached for the blanket and covered her over to save her further embarrassment. She checked her arms, neck and head. 'I can't feel any broken bones, which is a good sign.' She placed her fingers in Grace's palms. 'Can you squeeze my fingers, please?'

Grace was able to do so on both sides.

'Good.'

'Ambulance is pulling into the theme park now,' someone said.

'Good.' Rachael glanced at Joe. 'Is there anyone else who needs attention?'

'Ivan?' Joe called.

'I heard. I'll check around.'

'Thanks.' They stayed with Grace until the paramedics came over. Rachael smiled as she recognised Smitty. 'Back so soon?' She stood up to meet him.

'Can't keep me away.'

'How's Wong?' Joe asked urgently.

'They whisked him to Theatre to try and find the source of the bleeding. What do you need here?'

Rachael had just done Grace's obs and reported her findings. 'Tonic-clonic seizure. She's stable but needs oxygen and an IV line. Glasgow coma scale is 15. Patient has voided and is highly embarrassed by the whole episode.'

'Not surprising.' Smitty nodded.

'I've given her phenytoin, which should see her through until she's at the hospital.'

'Right. Everything settled here now?' Smitty glanced around at the scene in general.

'We're just waiting for Ivan to give us an update. Once it's clear, we'll follow you to the hospital.'

'I'll get Grace into the ambulance,' Smitty replied.

Rachael helped Smitty get Grace ready for transfer as Joe went to speak to Ivan. 'How are you feeling now?' she asked her patient.

'Stupid.' Grace closed her eyes.

'That's natural. Smitty here's going to take good care of you and I'll catch up with you at the hospital. All right?'

'Yes.' Grace closed her eyes as the stretcher was put into the ambulance.

Rachael looked around for Joe who was headed in their direction. 'All clear?'

'All clear,' he acknowledged. 'We'll see you at the hospital,' he told Smitty, before looking at Rachael. 'Let's go.'

She nodded. 'I'll get my bag.' She collected it and said goodbye to Ivan, thanking him for looking after Declan.

'My pleasure. As I said, anything for Joe and his family.'

Rachael was still smiling as she and Joe walked out to the parking lot. 'Where's your car?' he asked.

'My mum drove it to her house.'

Joe's only answer was to raise an enquiring eyebrow. Rachael decided to ignore it. They walked over to a green Jaguar. She glanced at the number plate and this time it was her turn to raise an eyebrow.

'JOE-19.' She smiled. 'I think you're a little older than that, Joe.'

Joe frowned as he unlocked the door and held hers open. 'Nineteen's my lucky number.' He waited until she was seated before heading around to the driver's side.

'That's it? Nineteen's your lucky number?'

He shrugged. 'A lot happened when I was nineteen.'

The smile slid from Rachael's face. 'Yes. Yes, it did.' She wanted to ask him all the questions that had been floating around in her head, she wanted to sort out the past, to try and make sense of it, but her mother's words about focusing on the here and now slipped into her mind and she forced herself to take a deep, relaxing breath.

'Thank you,' she said, after he'd started the engine and pulled out onto the road.

'For?'

'For being nice to Declan.'

He smiled. 'It's not hard.'

'Still, it means a lot to me, Joe.' She twisted her hands together in her lap, amazed to feel her heart rate start to increase. She took another deep breath, trying to steady her mounting nerves. A few minutes of silence passed. 'Joe.'

'Hmm?'

'I know you said you wanted to spend time alone with Declan and I appreciate that. I'm all for it but…' She closed her eyes, unable to look at him as she spoke just in case he turned her down. 'But would you also like to spend time alone with me?'

Joe glanced at her so suddenly the car swerved slightly. 'Er…uh…sure.' He cleared his throat.

'You don't sound too convinced.'

'No. It's not that. It's just…you caught me by surprise.'

'Oh. So you're open to the idea, then?'

He stopped the car at a red light and turned to look at her. Even beneath the artificial lights outside, it was still difficult to see all of his face, but she hoped his gaze was filled with delight at the prospect.

'Yes. Rach, I'm a little astounded that you needed to ask.'

She shrugged, feeling a little foolish. It had been easier when he hadn't been watching her so intently, and she wished for the light to change so she could escape once more into the dark. 'I'm not saying we jump straight into bed if that's what you're thinking.'

His grin was immediate and wolfish. 'Hey, I wouldn't be

a red-blooded male if I didn't admit the thought had already crossed my mind, but I understand what you mean.'

The light turned and he resumed driving. 'I know we still have a lot of things to work out, but it would be nice to just spend some time together. The two of us. Grab a cup of coffee or something.'

'Or something.' He nodded.

Rachael sighed with relief and he chuckled at the sound. 'Surely it wasn't that bad, asking me that question.'

'Of course it was. You have been known to turn me down before.'

'Cheap shot,' he said good-naturedly.

'Yes, it was. I apologise.' She was glad to see he'd lost his black mood from the movie set. Perhaps she'd imagined it and had misinterpreted the dark looks he'd given her. 'I'm glad you're the one driving to the hospital. I would have got lost by now.'

Joe smiled as he turned off for the hospital and parked the Jaguar in the doctors' car park. Rachael grabbed her bag and walked quickly beside him into the hospital, bumping into Smitty again.

'What took you so long?' He grinned at both of them and then held up his hands. 'No. On second thought, don't tell me. I don't want to know.'

'Where's Grace?' Joe asked, ignoring Smitty's teasing words.

'Examination cubicle four, and Rino's at X-Ray.'

'Wong?'

'Still in surgery.'

'Thanks.'

'All part of the service. That should be it for me tonight. I'll catch you folks later.'

Joe guided Rachael over to the nurses' station.

'Oh, so you're Joe's partner. He told us you'd be in at some time. I guess you didn't expect to be here so soon.'

'I'll be in EC-4. Come in when you're done.' Joe went to check on Grace.

'I'm not his partner, just the locum working at his private practice,' Rachael corrected the nurse.

'Whatever. You'll need to fill in some forms, but if you wanted to check out the tonic-clonic patient first, she's in EC-4. The paperwork can wait.' The nurse held out her hand for Rachael's bag. 'I'll lock it in the drawer here.'

'Thanks.' She headed for EC-4 and felt strange pulling back the curtain when she really felt like knocking.

'Rachael.' Grace's gaze fell on her with relief. The oxygen mask was still in place and an IV line was in her arm.

'Finished already?' He raised a teasing eyebrow. 'Come in, come in.'

Joe gave Rachael an updated report on Grace's vital signs and she was pleased to hear everything was fine. 'I was just about to order a few tests for Grace. What do you think, Rach?'

'EEG definitely, and compare it with the one she had three months ago. ECG, full blood work-up and urine analysis.' She shrugged. 'For a start.'

'Good.' Joe nodded to the nurse. 'Can you get them organised please, Beatrice?'

'Sure thing, Joe.'

'Good. We'll be back to check on you later, Grace. You rest and take it easy.'

'Yes, Joe.' Grace smiled as she closed her eyes. 'At least I can try, before they start poking and prodding me.'

They both smiled and headed out the cubicle. 'Are you the treating doctor?'

'Studio rules. All patients from the movie set are admitted under my name, even though several specialists may see them.' He walked over to the nurses' station and picked up the phone. A moment later, he asked the switchboard to page the neurology registrar. 'Although Wong is in surgery with all different kinds of specialists looking after him, I'm the one who coordinates everything because I'm the one who has to write reports for the studio's insurers.'

'Sounds like fun.'

'Oh, it really isn't.' He smiled. 'Let's go find Rino.' She followed him to Radiology and was pleased when they found Rino had just finished there.

'Spine's not busted,' he said. 'Told you.'

'Yes, you did.' They chatted with Rino until the first lot of films came back. 'They're looking good. Nice clean break of the clavicle.' Joe accepted the next lot of films. 'Only your left tibia is fractured, but right side has both tib and fib. Due to the lacerations on your left leg, Zac will probably opt to put an external fixator on that one.'

'Zac?' Rachael asked.

'Orthopaedic surgeon,' Rino supplied. 'Open reduction and internal fixation on the right side?'

'Probably,' Joe responded, as he held the films up to the light so they could all see.

'Ever thought of going into medicine, Rino?' Rachael asked. 'You certainly know more than the average bloke.'

'You pick things up when you've been breaking bones all your life,' Joe teased.

'Not *all* my life, mate, but since I got into stunt work— yeah, quite a bit.'

Joe's pager beeped. 'Theatre,' he said, glancing at the extension number.

'Wong?' Rachael asked.

'Yes. I asked them to page me when they had news.' His face grew grim and the pain Rachael saw there, the deep-seated concern he had for his friend, made her heart melt. She reached out and squeezed his hand encouragingly.

'Go and find out.' She waited with Rino, neither of them speaking. She knew everything was all right the instant Joe returned.

'They've managed to stop the bleeding and he's turned the corner, but the general surgeon said it was touch and go for a while.'

Rachael breathed a sigh of relief and smiled at Rino. The look of guilt that had plagued the stunt driver from the instant she'd seen him had now eased.

'He's going to be fine,' Rachael said to Rino.

'Yeah.'

'Come on, Rach. I think it's coffee time.' Joe looked at Rino. 'Want one?'

'Nah, mate. I'm fine with the shot of pethidine I've had.'

'Suit yourself.' They headed back towards A and E, and when they passed the nurses' station, Beatrice grabbed Joe.

'Did you page the neurology registrar?'

'Yes. Oops.'

'How many times do I have to tell you? If you page someone, stay by the phone until they answer or at least tell someone you've done it and why!'

'Sorry.'

'I presumed it was for Grace.'

'Yes.'

'Well, wait here for three minutes and she'll meet you.'

'OK, but I'll just take—'

'No. You'll stay there, Joe Silvermark,' Beatrice commanded.

'Yes. I'll stay here.' He nodded meekly and Rachael couldn't help but laugh. 'Go and sit in the doctors' tearoom. I'll be there soon.'

'I can wait with you.'

'Rachael!' he said in exasperation.

'All right. Have it your own way.' He gave her directions and she found the room without difficulty. She sat down and put her feet up on another chair, tipping her head backwards as she pulled the braid from her hair and ran her fingers through it, untangling knots. She closed her eyes, feeling the tension of the past few hours began to ease.

It had been a long time since she'd been in an emergency situation like that. Not that it bothered her, just that she was out of practice. Once she was more settled here on the Gold Coast, she'd have to sign up for some GP refresher courses.

Sighing, she lifted her head and slowly opened her eyes. She jumped a little when she realised Joe was standing in the doorway, watching her intently.

'Everything organised?' She should probably sit up straight and take her feet off the chair, but she didn't have the energy.

'Yes. We'll have to get you registered here so you have the authority to admit patients if necessary.'

Rachael shrugged. 'Is there much point? I'll only be at your clinic until the end of next week.'

He frowned and went to sit down on the chair where her feet were. She quickly moved them, but after he'd sat down, he picked them up and placed them on his knee. Carefully he removed her shoes and began tenderly massaging her insteps.

Rachael groaned in pleasure and felt herself begin to melt. 'That feels *so* good.'

'I know.'

'You remember?'

'That you like having your feet massaged? Of course. The first time you let me touch you was to massage your feet on the bus trip.'

'Oh, yeah. I'd forgotten that.'

Joe chuckled. 'Most guys get to hold the girl's hand or put their arm around her shoulders, but me? No. I get to massage her very smelly feet.'

'They weren't smelly.'

'They were so.'

'Were not.'

'Were.'

She giggled. 'Yes, they were, yet you still did it.'

His smile was heart-melting and now he'd brought the topic up, she remembered just how quickly she'd melted beneath those megawatt smiles. 'I was trying to impress you.'

'It worked.'

'So it would seem.'

They both fell silent. 'What happened, Joe?'

'Tonight?'

'No.' She paused and looked into his eyes. 'To us.' She shook her head slowly. 'I still don't understand what happened and I've spent the past fifteen years trying to figure it out. As far as I could tell, one minute we were happily married and the next you were rushing me even faster towards the courthouse for the annulment.' Her words were soft yet filled with repressed hurt.

Joe's face became an unreadable mask. 'It wasn't meant to be, Rach.'

She bit her lip and looked down at her hands. They were clasped tightly together as she worked up the courage to ask her next question. Regardless of his answer, she needed to know, and she hoped this time, with fifteen years having passed, she'd get a different reply. 'Joe…' She swallowed nervously. 'Did you really mean it? What you said? That you'd only married me to get me into bed? That it had all been a joke?'

She held her breath, waiting…waiting for the words that would either make or break her.

CHAPTER SIX

JOE recalled the words with perfect clarity.

He recalled saying them to her with all the venom he'd been able to muster, and he'd felt sick to his stomach as he'd stood there and blatantly lied to her. Looking back—which he often had—he wished he'd handled the situation better, but he'd been a confused and idiotic nineteen-year-old who hadn't known any different.

Joe continued to massage her feet, searching for the right words.

'It's all right,' she said, when he didn't reply. 'Forget it.' She had her answer. His silence was her answer, and he was probably trying to find a nicer way of saying exactly what he'd said that morning. Amazingly, she could feel tears beginning to well and realised she needed to get out of there—as soon as possible!

As she went to remove her feet from his hands, he held onto them. 'No, Rach. You misunderstood my silence. I want to answer but I was trying to think of the best way to explain.' He shrugged. 'We were…young…naïve, impulsive.'

'You weren't naïve, Joe.'

He grimaced wryly. 'No, but you were, and I should never have taken advantage of you.'

'Was it true, though?'

'That I only suggested we get married to get you into bed? No. At the risk of sounding conceited, I would have been able to talk you into it if that had been my sole motive.'

She acknowledged his words with a slow nod. 'So you really did want to marry me? It wasn't a joke?'

After all this time, he knew he owed her the truth. 'No, Rachael. It wasn't a joke.'

A shuddering sob escaped her lips as she was swamped with relief. 'You have no idea how that's haunted me all these years. I'd go over everything in my head like a stuck record. What had I said? What had I done? It had to have been something to make you say such horrible things to me.'

'It wasn't you. You didn't do anything wrong.'

'Then why?'

'I needed to hurt you.'

'You succeeded, but *why*? Why, Joe?' This time, when he remained silent, Rachael slowly began to connect the dots. 'I got too close.' A look of dawning realisation crossed her face.

'*Way* too close.' He exhaled harshly and lifted her feet, tenderly placing them on the chair. He needed a bit more distance between them—even now, although this distance was more physical than emotional, he still needed it.

A nurse poked her head into the room. 'Anyone seen Tess Marshall?'

'No,' Joe replied, and the nurse left. 'This isn't the place for this discussion.'

'Then where? Come on, Joe. We can't just leave it at that. I want to get on with my life, to move forward, but it's just so hard to try and do that when the same questions that were buzzing around in my head fifteen years ago are still there—unanswered.'

'Closure.' He said the word with a nod. 'You're right. We do need to discuss this, but you have Declan waiting for you.'

'He's with my parents. He's fine.'

'Is he staying overnight with them?'

Rachael grimaced. 'No. He's had an extremely full day and usually, when that happens, his mind goes into overload. First going out with you, then bungee jumping, then the accident and helping out. It's a lot for his mind to absorb.'

'He's fourteen, Rach. Don't you think you're overreacting?'

Rachael sighed. 'Think back to when you were fourteen, Joe. You never really told me what your childhood was like but, after seeing where you were raised, I can imagine.'

He grimaced. 'I never wanted you to see that.'

'I know, but I did. As I was saying, remember the things you saw when you were Declan's age. I'm sure they were a lot worse than an accident on a movie set but, still, I'll bet when things didn't go the way you planned, all you wanted was for someone to be there for you. I'm not talking about psychoanalysing or anything like that but just having someone there. To feel that you weren't alone, even if you didn't talk. Someone to put their arms around you and just hold you without probing any further beneath the surface. Didn't you want that when you were fourteen, Joe?'

Joe looked down at the floor. How did she do that? Without him even realising, she just climbed right inside his head and read his mind. It hadn't been the first time it had happened and he realised now it wouldn't be the last. He shuffled his feet, then looked up at her. 'This really isn't the place.' He raked a hand through his hair. 'We should go somewhere else to talk, but I want to stay at the hospital.'

'For Wong.' She nodded. 'I understand.'

'You do, don't you? Somehow, by some miracle, you've always been able to understand me.'

'And that scares you?'

He gave a shout of laughter without humour and shook his head. 'Terrifies me, Rach.'

'And that's why you don't open up to me?'

'I find it hard to open up to anyone but you seem to have this imaginary can-opener and without my permission you get inside.'

'You make me sound like a parasite.'

'You know what I mean.'

'That irritates you, doesn't it? That I get in without permission?'

He turned to face her, his expression earnest. 'I'm a private person by nature, Rach. I'm not into deep relationships, but when I met you and you just seemed to…*get* me, I found myself in uncharted waters.'

'Out of your comfort zone.'

Joe nodded. 'Correct, and I'd taken great pains to have that comfort zone, to find a safe place within me.'

'Joe.' Rachael placed her hand on his arm and looked imploringly at him. 'I never wanted to hurt you, but even from the first moment we met you were an enigma to me. I probe because it helps me understand, and I'm one of those annoying people who needs to understand. Once I understand, I can cope.'

'Hence your current dilemma.'

'Yes. I don't understand why you pushed me away, but let me just say that everything I found out about you when we were together I loved.'

He nodded and took her hand in his. 'The way you spoke to me, the discussions we had… You made me feel smart. You made me feel as though I had worth. No one had ever made me feel that way.'

'Made you *feel* smart?' She smiled at him. 'Joe, you *are* smart. Where do you think Declan gets it from!'

'From both of us.' He reached out his free hand and caressed her cheek. 'You're a highly intelligent woman, Rach, and I could never figure out what it was you saw in me. I was just this loser who'd been raised in an abusive environment and who'd managed to scrape together enough money to get out of the country.'

'That's not what I saw.' When Joe raised his eyebrows she continued. 'I saw a man who knew how to let loose and have a good time. You were wild and exciting and the sexiest man I'd ever met.'

'You decided to slum it.'

'Is that what you think?' Rachael was astonished. 'Because you're wrong. Those were my first impressions of you, Joe. *Then* I got to know you and that's when I started falling in love. We may have initially been attracted to the external packages, but I've always believed we touched each other's souls.'

He couldn't help himself any longer and dragged her close to him. She didn't pull back or resist. Instead, he saw she welcomed the contact. Reaching up, she slowly brushed her fingers through his hair and he groaned at the touch.

'You get my blood pumping faster than any bungee jump or any of the other adrenaline rushes I've experienced over the years.'

Gently, she urged his head down and at the same time she rose up on her toes, the length of their bodies brushing firmly together. He breathed in deeply, the scent of wild berries over-powering him.

'You smell the same,' he whispered, his gaze fixed on her mouth. His hands sensually caressed her back in small circles the way he knew she liked. 'You feel the same.'

'Hurry up and kiss me,' she panted, and watched as the sexy smile she remembered tugged at his lips. Her stomach churned with longing and she was glad he was holding her tightly because she doubted her legs would be able to support her.

'You're still impatient, too.'

'Only with you.'

He continued to tease her by eluding her mouth and burying his face in her neck, filling his senses with her scent. He pressed kisses to her neck. 'You taste the same.'

'Joseph.' She growled his name and he chuckled lightly. Not giving him the chance to escape, she dug her hands into his hair, wrenched his head up and brought it down so their lips could meet… The moment they touched, she sighed with relief.

As ever, his mouth was masterful, knowing exactly how to bring a response from her. Her insides twirled with longing as the sensations continued to grow. Testing, teasing and tantalising… He wasn't going to let her get away with a quick, reuniting kiss—not that she'd want him to. It was as though he was taking his time to familiarise himself with the feel of her mouth beneath his, and she was in no mood to contradict him.

They moved in complete synchronicity, as though the past fifteen years hadn't happened. A reunion they'd both needed with the promise of what they knew lay beyond these heart-wrenching kisses.

With a short groan coming from deep in the back of his throat, he pulled back. 'Mmm. Definitely taste the same.'

'Shh,' was all she said as she dragged his mouth back to hers. This time she took control, desire pouring out of her as she led them both towards a journey they'd taken many years ago. They needed to build bridges, to fix the rift that had grown between them due to both life and circumstances, and she knew this was a sure-fire way to get the building process started…as well as being highly enjoyable.

Her mouth on his was eager and slightly desperate, almost willing him to come along for the ride. If he thought he could tease and nibble, he had another think coming. The impatience she'd felt earlier was nothing compared to how she felt now. The moment seemed to slow down, time seemed to stand still. She waited for him to accept and appreciate her efforts.

She didn't have to wait long.

After a heart-splitting second, his mouth was roving over hers in that hot and hungry way she recalled. The passion, the fire, the heat—it was there, and it was as raw and untamed as it had been when they'd been teenagers. How could the need which had lain so dormant in her suddenly spring to life with such fever? A fever she knew was highly infectious to only one other person—and he was showing the same symptoms.

Ever since she'd first seen him again, her heart had acknowledged the inevitability of this moment, even though her head had denied it. They were meant for each other and right now neither one disagreed.

Where there had previously been apprehension and uncertainty between them, they were now both confident to take the frightening natural attraction which still existed to the next level. On and on the fire continued to rage within them as their mouths hungrily explored and remembered.

'Rachael!' He finally pulled back, both of them panting from lack of air. They'd been completely caught up in each other, neither wanting to be the one to break the contact. Breathing had completely slipped their minds until it had been imperative they part. He sucked in a breath and pressed his lips onto hers, knowing with absolute certainty she would respond.

'You're so…captivating,' he whispered brokenly as his mouth still took hungrily from hers. 'So…vibrant and alive, and if I don't stop myself soon, I'm not going to be able to.' He was talking more to himself than her, but didn't mind she was in on his thoughts.

He had the most sexy, desirable and passionate woman he'd ever known right here in his arms, and he was hard-pressed not to scoop her up and find somewhere soft to lay her down. He even glanced around at their surroundings, hoping to find a bed had miraculously appeared—but it hadn't.

He chuckled and gathered her close, pressing kisses to the top of her head. 'Unbelievable.'

'Isn't it?' She sighed and listened as his erratic heart rate slowly began to return to a normal rhythm.

'I can't believe it's still there. So strong, so…'

'Encompassing.'

'Yes.' He pulled back to gaze down into her face and couldn't resist brushing his lips once more across hers. 'How could you think I wouldn't want to spend time alone with you—especially when we have *this* between us?'

Rachael chuckled and accepted another kiss. 'I'm allowed my own insecurities, Joe.'

'Well, not about me wanting you because, believe me, Rach, I do.' His pager beeped and he released her so he could check the number. 'Theatre,' he said, and went to the phone on the wall, quickly dialling the relevant extension.

'It's Joe,' he said a moment later. 'How's Wong?'

'Everything's going fine,' Zac reported. 'The general surgeons have finished and the urology surgeon is with him now. I have his X-rays back if you wanted to come and have a look.'

'We're in the tearoom.'

'We?' Zac asked. 'I certainly hope this "we" you're referring to involves a beautiful woman.'

'It does.'

'Good. I look forward to meeting her.'

Joe disconnected the call, a silly schoolboy grin on his face at the thought he could show 'his girl' to his mate.

'How is he?'

'Who? Zac?'

'Don't be obtuse, Silvermark.' The fact that he was joking meant things were better than he'd expected.

'Oh. Wong.' Joe passed on the details as he crossed back to her side. 'Want to go look at some X-rays?'

'You're such a party animal and always know how to show a girl a good time,' she teased.

'Be quiet and come here.' He pulled her into the circle of his arms once more and pressed his mouth to hers. Rachael made no move to pull away but instead sighed and snuggled closer to him, her arms about his waist, her eyes closed.

'Joe? Don't we need to go?'

His answer was to kiss her again.

'This isn't helping, Joe.'

'Mmm. I don't know about you but I'm feeling quite fine.'

'Come on.' She pressed a kiss to his lips but couldn't bring herself to end the embrace.

'You're right,' he growled, but even though he spoke the words, he still didn't move.

'You first.'

'You don't play fair.'

Rachael chuckled. 'We're doctors. Since when is life fair?' She opened her eyes and pulled back to look at him. Joe immediately brushed his lips against hers once more.

'I can't get enough of you.'

'The feeling is very mutual.' She moved away slightly and reluctantly he let her go. Rachael reached for his hand and turned it over in both of hers before saying softly, 'What's next, Joe?' She glanced up at him, her expression filled with concern.

'For us? Honestly? I don't know.' He laced their fingers together and gave her hand a little squeeze. 'For now, though, let's have a look at Wong's X-rays.'

Rachael nodded and together they headed out of the tea-room. 'Hey, wait a minute. Don't I still need to fill in some paperwork? Can I just go looking at X-rays and giving my opinion—if I'm asked—if I'm not licensed to work here?'

'It's just X-rays, Rachael. Not espionage. You can fill them in any time tonight because they won't be processed until tomorrow morning, but at least the red tape will be covered.'

'OK. Well, perhaps I should get them out of the way now.'

Joe indulged her and they walked over to the nurses' station where Beatrice handed over the forms to register Rachael as a visiting medical officer. Rachael noticed the glances a few of the staff gave them due to the fact that Joe was still holding her hand and realised hospitals around the world were the same—the staff living off rumours and gossip. She felt like grabbing Joe and planting a big, smoochy kiss on his lips just to ensure the rumours could be confirmed.

'What are you thinking, Rach?' Joe asked quietly as he waited for her to complete the forms.

'Why?'

'You have that teasing look in your eyes. That usually means you're up to no good.'

She glanced at him, doing her best 'who me?' look.

'Yes, Miss Sweetness-and-Light. *You*,' he answered, then chuckled. 'You're conscious that people are watching us together and you're thinking about teasing them.'

Rachael fumbled with what she'd been writing before putting the pen down and staring at him in amazement. Joe straightened up from where he'd been leaning against the desk. 'You mean I'm right?'

'I know we used to be able to read each other's minds, Joe, but this is ridiculous.'

Joe preened like a peacock and Rachael rolled her eyes. He edged closer. 'Let's give them something to talk about.'

Before she could say or do anything, he leaned over and placed his mouth on hers. It wasn't a brief kiss, as she'd expected, but a slow, intimate kiss, his lips slightly open with just a hint of tongue. Soft, sensual and simply seductive. When he pulled back, she saw the desire in his eyes.

'That ought to do the trick,' he murmured, and straightened, getting himself under control.

Rachael cleared her throat and glanced around them. As the nurses went about their business, she knew several had witnessed the kiss. One or two glared daggers at her, a few others had dreamy, romantic looks on their faces. She even heard one of them sigh with longing.

'Trying to scare someone off?'

'Rachael.' He placed a hand over his heart. 'I'm highly offended you should think that.'

'I know you too well, Joseph Silvermark.' She completed the forms.

'When did I ever use you to scare other women off, as you put it?'

'Hmm. Let me think. There was Janice and Celeste, not to mention Freya and Samantha.'

'When?'

'On the tour, Joe. You knew they all had the hots for you.'

The peacock returned as he preened. 'Really? All of them?'

Rachael laughed and shook her head. 'I need to go ring my parents to let them know what's happening.'

Joe sobered immediately. 'And to check on Declan.'

'It's a mother's prerogative.'

'OK, Dr Cusack.' He handed her the phone from the nurses' desk. 'Dial zero to get an outside line.'

'Thank you, Dr Silvermark.'

'What?' Beatrice was astounded. 'You're still on a last-name basis after a kiss like that?'

Both of them laughed.

'I'll go get the X-rays and meet you back in the doctors' tearoom,' Joe said, giving her some privacy.

'OK.' Rachael dialled the number, watching Joe hungrily as he walked away. He had such a nice back with those wonderful broad shoulders. Years ago she'd touched every inch of him and had tenderly caressed the scars he had on his arms and back. She had her theory as to how he'd come across them, but even now the urge to kiss every single one better was growing stronger by the minute.

Declan answered the phone, bringing her back to the present. 'Hi, Mum. How's Wong? And how's the stunt guy?'

'Wong's still in Theatre but apparently things are progressing well, and Rino should be waiting to go into surgery.'

'Then everyone's good, eh?'

'Yes.' She heard her son sigh with relief. 'Are you all right?'

'I'm fine, Mum.' His tone was bored.

'OK. We may be a little while longer but not too much.'

'And Joe's going to drive you back here, right?'

'That's right.'

'Can I see him?'

'You might be asleep.'

'Please, Mum.' The pleading tone was back. 'I just want to see the guy. That's all.'

'OK. When we get to Grandma's, I'll ask him to come in to see you.'

'Excellent.'

'So long as you try and get some sleep to start off with. You have school tomorrow.'

'Yes, Mother.' Again his tone was bored. 'So we're going back to the hotel tonight?'

'Yes.'

'OK. I'll have everything ready by the door.'

Rachael rang off, her thoughts on Declan. She'd heard the tension in his voice no matter how much he'd tried to disguise it. There would be hardly any sleep for either of them tonight and she wasn't looking forward to it.

She saw Joe come out of the emergency theatre block with another doctor in scrubs. The man was a similar height and build to Joe, and she surmised it must be his friend Zac. The two men were talking and when Zac gave Joe a playful thump on the shoulder and glanced over her way, she realised she was the topic of their conversation.

Taking a deep breath, she headed over.

'Declan OK?'

'He's fine.'

'Rachael, this is Zac.'

Zac's smile was teasing, his blue eyes twinkling with repressed humour. '*Very* pleased to meet you, Rachael.' They headed for the doctors' tearoom.

'Likewise.' She paused for a moment. 'Is there some joke I'm missing?'

'No,' Joe said.

'Yes,' Zac said in unison, then chuckled. 'Not a joke, really. Just that I told Joe not so long ago that a person's past has a way of catching up with them and…well…here you are.' At Rachael's confused frown, Zac explained. 'The same thing happened to me. The woman I dated in med school came to work here six years ago and we were reunited. We had a lot of stuff to work through, naturally—hence my crack about the past catching up with you, especially if you lock it away and refuse to deal with it—but work through it we did and we've been happily married since.'

Rachael smiled sincerely. 'I'm glad.' Her opinion of Zac grew immensely because if he knew she was part of Joe's past, it meant here was another person Joe trusted.

'Anyway, let's not get into everything now—except I will say that Julia will definitely want to meet you.'

'Your wife?'

'Yes. She's off on maternity leave at the moment.' Zac preened. 'We've just had a baby girl. Four months old and looks just like her mother. We'll have to arrange for you, Joe and your son to come over some time.'

Rachael glanced at Joe, not sure how he felt about all this, but as he wasn't jumping in to say anything, she decided to wing it. 'Thanks.'

'Let's take a look at these X-rays,' was Joe's only comment, and Rachael realised he was distancing himself again…running, protecting himself because he was once more out of his depth. They studied the films and Rachael wasn't surprised to see that Wong's pelvis was fractured in three different places.

'He's busted up his left leg quite badly.' Zac hooked up a new X-ray beside the pelvic one. 'I'll do the Grosse and

LUCY CLARK 113

Kempf intramedullary nailing down his left femur soon, but the tibia and fibula can wait for another twenty-four hours.'

'And the pelvis?'

'I'll monitor it over the next week because the posterior fracture up here…' he pointed to the fracture in the bone '…may actually heal itself and not require surgical intervention. Besides, it also gives his other abdominal injuries time to heal before he's being poked and prodded there again.'

'You'll call me when he's done in Theatre?'

'Yes.' Zac took the films down and slid them back into the X-ray sleeve as his pager beeped. He checked the extension. 'Theatre two. Looks like they're ready for Rino.'

'You're operating on him now?'

'Yes. We'll fix his right tibia and fibula with ORIF and, depending on when I need to go into surgery with Wong, I might put Rino's external fixator on his left tibia tomorrow. I'll see what the time constraints are.'

'He was right.' Rachael nodded, telling Zac that Rino had known exactly how his legs would be fixed. 'What about his clavicle?'

'I'll strap it, which is going to be highly uncomfortable for him but, hey, I guess that's the price he pays for being a stuntman.'

'It's in his blood.' Joe shrugged.

Zac agreed. 'Hey, you guys look exhausted. Get out of here and go see your son. You know what hospitals are like. If you hang around here for too long, an emergency will come in and you'll be stuck here for hours.'

'Get out while the going's good, eh?' Joe smiled for the first time since he'd introduced Zac to Rachael. 'Good thinking. Take care of Rino and—'

'Let you know what happens in Theatre?' Zac grinned at his friend. 'Will do. Oh, and I'll get Jules to give you a call and fix up a date for dinner.'

'No hurry,' Joe replied as he ushered Rachael out the tearoom. Although he was still smiling as he said the words, the smile didn't quite meet his eyes. It spoke volumes to her and she realised Joe was quite a few steps behind her. Where she knew her love for him had never died, he was still floundering in the dark and running as fast as he could every time a new emotion assailed him.

They checked on Grace, who'd been admitted to the neurology department and was stable. She was sleeping so they headed to the nurses' station to talk to the registrar. 'EEG doesn't tell us much,' the neurology registrar said. 'I'll book her in for a MRI and see what that tells me.'

Joe nodded. 'You know she was in an accident three months ago?'

'I read the notes you wrote, Joe.'

'Just checking.'

'Was she involved in the stunt tonight?'

'No. In fact, she was working the clapperboard.'

'The what?'

'The board that marks the scene on the roll of film.'

'Oh. So she wasn't involved with the stunt tonight?'

'No.'

'Well, thanks to the immediate medical attention, Grace has a good chance of recovery. The question is, will she fit again? That's what we need to determine.'

'Good. I'll catch up with you tomorrow when you know more.' Joe and Rachael said goodbye, stopping by the nurses' station to collect her bag.

'I guess we'll be seeing you around,' Beatrice said to Rachael. Rachael merely smiled and followed Joe as they headed for the exit. The cool autumn air hit Rachael as they walked out of the hospital.

'It's getting cold.'

'That's because it's almost midnight.'

She shook her head. 'Now I remember why I went into private practice.'

'Hospital life's not your scene?'

'Not really. Yours?'

Joe shrugged. 'I like it now and then, a bit of action, but every day?' He shook his head, answering his own question.

'So you get your action from the movie shoots.'

'Yes. Gives me variety, otherwise I'd get bored.'

'Mmm-hmm.' She nodded knowingly.

'What?' he asked defensively.

'You're always looking for the next challenge.'

'So?'

'I'm not criticising, Joe. It's actually quite normal for people with higher-than-average IQs to have that urge.'

He rolled his eyes as they walked to his car. 'How many books have you read on this subject?'

'Quite a few. I've had to so I could learn the most effective way to deal with Declan.'

'Have you ever thought he'd be just fine without all the labels being put on him?'

'I've already told you I don't like the labels but the truth is, I've *needed* to learn. Joe, think back to when you were at school and the work was so boring. You could understand what the teacher was getting at before she'd finished writing the question up on the board. You felt they were almost insulting you asking you to sit there and do such pathetic work. I know that happened to you, even though you've never said one word about it to me. Then I'll bet you started playing up in class and getting into trouble. They labelled you, Joe, but not as gifted. No, they labelled you as a troublemaker who couldn't be bothered with hard work.'

She waited for him to unlock the door then climbed in the passenger seat, watching him walk around to the driver's side and get in. She could tell her words were beginning to affect him as his body language became defensive.

'How do you know all this?'

'From reading the books, Joe, and from seeing it happen

with Declan. I was called to the principal's office on his first week at school—he was five years old—and was told that my son was a troublemaker. He played up in class, he couldn't be bothered doing the work.'

'Really? What did you do?'

'I tried talking to Declan. He told me things were too easy. That's when I read my first book and realised it was up to me to do something about it. I asked to see the work they were giving him and eventually got the wheels in motion so Declan was challenged. Once he was working at the right level, he stopped misbehaving.' She paused. 'Don't you wish you'd had someone in your corner back when you started school? I know you didn't, and I'm not trying to resurrect old wounds, but I take my responsibilities as a parent seriously, and if other people think I'm an overreacting, neurotic mother, then so be it. It's better than being a mother who neglects her child's intellect.' She was past caring what other people thought of her but for some reason she desperately wanted Joe's approval. Still, as she'd spoken, she'd felt him tense, and when he glanced at her, she could see the shutters were already in place.

'You really get going on the subject, don't you?' His words were light, showing he wanted to keep this conversation on a more superficial level.

Rachael sighed and rubbed her temples. 'I guess.'

Joe started the engine and drove out of the car park and onto the road. 'Where to?'

She gave him her parents' address and he said he knew the area. It was an affluent area and the old feeling of inadequacy swamped him. He shook it away, telling himself circumstances had changed, and if he wanted to buy a house in the same area, he could well afford to.

Neither of them spoke for a few minutes and she began to feel the weight of the day catch up with her. Leaning her head back, she closed her eyes and sighed again, this time forcing her body to relax.

'I don't mean to preach, Joe, and don't worry that I'm going to psychoanalyse you because I'm not. I'm just trying to let you know how it is with Declan.'

'I appreciate it.'

'Really?' She turned her head so she could see him better. 'Why?'

'Why? Because he's my son and I've missed the first fourteen years of his life.'

'Yes.' She could feel the defensiveness start to kick in again. 'But you can hardly blame me for that.'

'I'm not looking to cast blame. I'm merely stating a fact.' He gripped the wheel as he continued to drive. He also didn't like the fact Rachael knew everything about the boy, whereas he'd barely scratched the surface. Declan was his son! He had a son! A son who was so like him in many respects it scared him. Joe wanted to show the kid how to loosen up a bit, to have some fun, smell the roses, and he knew if he voiced those thoughts out loud, Rachael would take it as a criticism, which it wasn't.

It made him think that if he'd been around while Declan had been growing up, perhaps he wouldn't be having nightmares at the age of fourteen. Joe felt it was a kick in the gut to male pride to still be having bad dreams at such an age. That only happened to little kids. He surmised that Rachael called them nightmares because she didn't want to face that Declan was fast becoming a man. During the next few years, that's exactly what would happen, and Joe felt a sense of pride at the thought.

Paternal pride? Where had that come from, and so quickly? He'd only found out about Declan less than forty-eight hours ago and already he was feeling *pride*?

Joe turned into her parents' street and started checking the house numbers. It was then he noticed Rachael's eyes were closed and her face relaxed as she dozed. Something twisted in his gut at seeing her sitting there, so peaceful, so lovely.

Spotting her car sitting in a driveway, he stopped at the kerb outside the large house. He knew it was her car as it had been parked out the back at his private practice. At least…he *thought* it was her car. He'd better check but he took a moment just to sit there and look at her. Eventually he whispered, 'Rachael?'

'Mmm?' She sighed and tried to snuggle into the seat a bit more.

A slow smiled crossed his face, remembering how wonderful it had felt to have her snuggle into him, his arms securely around her as their heart rates had slowly returned to normal. His Rachael. The smile disappeared. That had been so long ago. He may have thought about her almost every day since they'd parted, but that didn't mean a thing. They were two different people now…two very different people…who just happened to have a son in common. He didn't know where his relationship with Declan was going. And Rachael? He was at an even bigger loss.

He wouldn't deny the attraction was still there, as potent and strong as ever, but that didn't mean a thing. Life could change—that was one lesson he'd learned early on. Clearing his throat, he gently put his hand on her shoulder and shook her.

'Rachael. We're here. Wake up.'

'Hmm?' She opened her eyes and, without moving, scanned her surroundings. Next, she jolted upright so quickly the seat belt restrained her.

'Take it easy.' The smile came naturally to his lips. 'We're here. At your parents' house.'

'Oh. Sorry. I must have dozed off.'

'Not surprising.' He took the keys out of the ignition and climbed out of the car. Rachael grabbed her bag and followed.

'This is a big enough place,' Joe said softly. 'Why aren't you staying here?'

'Because I don't want to take my parents for granted.'

'I doubt they'd think that.'

'That's not the point, Joe. They already do far too much for me and my dad's health isn't the best at the moment. I didn't want to add to his stress.'

'Fair enough.'

They walked across the front lawn and the sensor light came on. As Rachael didn't have her keys, she knocked lightly on the door and waited for someone to answer it. A moment later, her mother opened the door and beckoned them in. When Joe hesitated on the doorstep, Rachael turned and reached for his hand. 'Declan wanted to see you.'

'Oh.' Again, that pleasure and pride filled his heart and he almost felt like puffing out his chest.

'Yes. Come on.'

'Hi,' Elizabeth said, belting her robe around her waist and yawning. 'I'm just going to get my slippers,' she said, and disappeared again.

Joe closed the door behind him and they walked quietly through the house. 'Where is he?'

'He said he'd try and wait up but I think he might have given in to sleep. At least, I hope he has.' She pointed to the lounge room. 'This way.'

Sure enough, there was Declan, sprawled out on the couch, the TV still on, headphones on the floor. Rachael headed over to pick them up and turn the set off when she realised Declan was whimpering, his body twitching.

'No!' All the maternal love she had for her son welled to the surface as the twitching became more insistent. She knelt down and placed her hand on his forehead. 'He's sweating. Declan,' she said in her normal voice. 'Wake up.'

'Mum!' His eyes snapped open and he glanced wildly around the room as though he was searching for her. *'No!'*

The sound was wrenched from him and he sat up and hugged his knees to his chest. 'It's too much. It's too much. I can't do it.'

'Declan.' Rachael knew she had to keep her cool. 'It's all right. I'm here.' She put her hand on his arm but he flinched. She persisted, focusing all her attention on her son, vaguely registering that her mother had rushed into the room.

'It's too much,' he moaned with anguish.

'I know.' Rachael sat beside him and held him firmly, not letting him push her away this time. 'It's all right, darling. I'm here. Let it out. Don't hold onto it, Dec. Let it out, darling.'

When the gut-wrenching sobs came, Joe felt his own eyes fill with tears as he watched his son. Rachael was holding him, murmuring soothing words, and slowly the tears subsided. Joe swallowed the lump in his throat as he turned away and walked out of the room.

CHAPTER SEVEN

JOE'S whole body was tense with a pain he'd never experienced before. He pressed his fingers to his carotid pulse and was surprised to find it pounding fiercely. He raked his fingers through his hair, unable to get the image of Declan's wild gaze out of his mind. That was his son and his son was hurting. The urge to protect, to take away the pain, to hold his boy was so overwhelming, he thought he'd choke on the emotion.

Rachael had said Declan had nightmares, but what he'd just witnessed—what he could still hear as Declan continued to sob—was a boy going through pure anguish. What caused them? Why hadn't he woken up when Rachael had called his name? Joe roughly pushed the tears away and took out his handkerchief to blow his nose.

'Devastating, isn't it?' Elizabeth spoke softly from behind him and Joe spun to face her. The woman's eyes were wet with unshed tears and he realised she was in the same boat as him—onlooker and feeling completely helpless to make any difference. 'He doesn't have them as frequently now he's older, so I guess that's a positive.' She held out her hand. 'I'm Elizabeth.'

'I'm—'

'You're Joe.' She nodded. 'It's nice to finally meet you. The sobs have stopped, which means he's settling. Poor child gets awfully embarrassed if anyone sees him like that. We can go back in.' She headed into the room and Joe was left to follow which he did…hesitantly.

Rachael hadn't moved and neither had Declan. 'He's gone back to sleep,' she whispered when she saw them.

'Good. Do you want to stay here for the night?' Elizabeth asked.

Rachael shook her head. 'Thanks, Mum, but Declan wanted to see Joe and then return to the hotel so while it's more hectic to do that, I think we'll stick with the original plan.'

'OK, darling.' She kissed her daughter's head. 'You both look done in. Why don't I make some tea?' Before anyone could answer, Elizabeth had disappeared into the kitchen.

'Can you grab me that cushion over there? My back's starting to ache.'

Joe obliged and put the pillow behind her back so she could lean on the arm of the couch, shifting Declan and herself into a more comfortable position. 'Thanks. You may as well sit down.'

'You're not going to wake him?'

'Not yet. If I can get him back to sleep, he usually doesn't remember them. Do you mind? I'd like to give him another fifteen minutes if possible.'

'Uh…sure. Sure.' Joe sat in the armchair opposite her and raked a hand through his hair. 'So was that a mild one?'

Rachael smiled tiredly at his naivety. 'It's not a seizure, Joe, and they're all about the same intensity. I guess it depends on how long it takes me to get to him.'

'And what if you're not around?'

'I usually am. Tonight was a one-off and I don't think he'd been upset for too long.'

'How do you know?'

'Well, for a start, we would have heard him when we walked in the door and, also, it didn't take me too long to calm him down.'

'So this is the main reason you've opted for private practice?'

'Yes. It meant, as a general rule, that I could work normal hours while he was growing up.'

'You would have made a good surgeon.'

'I would have been bored. At least with general practice I get variety.'

'How many varieties of flu are there?'

Rachael laughed. 'Good point.' She sobered. 'Thanks for hanging around.'

'No problem.'

'Are you all right?'

'Me?' He waved away her concern. 'Don't worry about me.'

'It's scary, Joe. It's scary to watch your child go through any pain.'

'So I'm beginning to realise,' he mumbled, giving in to the fact that Rachael could read him like a book. 'How often does he have them?'

Rachael shrugged slightly. 'Usually when too much has happened. I can't say I'm surprised he's had one, after the past few days. Meeting you, spending time with you, starting a new school, going to the movie set.'

'The bungee jump, being introduced to so many new people, me thinking he needed more fun in his life.' Joe hung his head in shame. 'Rach, I'm so sorry.'

'It's not your fault, Joe. Declan wanted to do the bungee jump and it's good for him to meet new people, and he does need to have more fun. Maybe not all in one day…' She smiled as she trailed off.

'I didn't realise this would happen.'

'Leave it, Joe. Trust me, there's no point beating yourself up about the past. Unfortunately for Declan, this is something he needs to learn to manage. He has to realise when he's overloaded and pace himself.'

Joe watched as Declan shifted, sprawling out and raising his arm above his head so it fell across Rachael's face. 'Dec!' She laughed and pushed his arm away, then sighed. 'I hate to think what's going to happen when girls come into his life.'

'Oh, yeah!' Joe's eyes widened. 'I hadn't thought of that.'

'It's the time in a boy's life when he needs his father, Joe.'

'You want me to give him advice about girls?'

'No.' Rachael laughed. 'That's not what I meant. I just meant…you know…he'll be needing that male influence and I don't think my dad's up to it.'

'Discussing the birds and the bees?' Joe raked a hand through his hair again and, unable to sit still any longer, stood and walked around the room.

'He knows about the birds and the bees. In fact, we've already had some very interesting discussions about…body changes.'

Joe groaned and shook his head.

'Here's the tea,' Elizabeth said cheerfully as she carried the tray into the dimly lit room. Rachael realised at some point her mother had switched off the television, coiled up the headphones cable and turned on a side lamp.

'Perfect timing,' Joe commented, and Rachael laughed again. She accepted the cup her mother handed her with thanks and watched as Elizabeth fussed over Joe.

'Now, do you prefer to be called Joe or Joseph?'

'Either.'

'Really?' Rachael was surprised and received a glare for her trouble. 'I didn't think you liked Joseph, that's all.'

'I think it's a nice name,' Elizabeth added.

'Then you may call me Joseph,' he said, still wary of Elizabeth but wanting to do whatever he could to help smooth any future contact he might have with her.

'Excellent.' They were all talking quietly but not whispering and Declan stirred a little. 'Oh, he's such a big lad. I can't believe how quickly he's grown.'

'Heavy, too.' Rachael sipped her tea before holding her cup out of the way as one of Declan's hands came towards her again. 'Take this, please, Joe. I think I'll wake him up before he whacks me in the face.' She waited until her hands were empty, then kissed the top of her son's head, glad his tem-

perature had returned to normal. 'Declan? Honey? Wake up.'
She touched his face and kissed his head once more. Unlike
before, he slowly stretched and this time his hand connected
with his mother's face. At the contact, he sat up.

'Mum! Sorry.'

'It's all right. I didn't need that cheekbone,' she joked.

Declan glanced around the room. 'Grandma. Joe!' His eyes
widened in surprise. 'What have you all been doing?
Watching me sleep?'

'You do it so well,' Rachael murmured, glad to have the
blood circulating around her body once more.

'What time is it?'

'Just after midnight.'

'Wow. You were a long time at the hospital.'

'You can say that again.'

'You were a long time at the hospital,' Declan said, smiling
at his mother.

Rachael chuckled and glanced at Joe. 'See? He definitely
has your warped sense of humour.'

Joe forced a smile. He was still shell-shocked by what had
happened to Declan, and now the three other people in the
room were behaving as though nothing was out of the ordinary. There was something wrong with his son! He didn't
know how to explain the sudden panic that seemed to con-
strict his chest, and he wasn't sure he could sit and make idle
chit-chat. His palms began to sweat and he felt as though the
room was closing in on him. He stood up abruptly, almost
spilling the cup of tea he'd forgotten he was holding, and
quickly put the cup back on the tray. 'I need to go.'

Rachael frowned at his sudden change. 'Joe?'

'Uh…early morning.'

'Are you going to be at the movie set again?' Declan asked
eagerly.

'Er…no. I'll take morning clinic so your mother can have
a rest.' The words tumbled out of his mouth and he realised

he'd do or say anything he had to, to get out of there as soon as possible.

'It's fine, Joe. I'll be at the clinic at the normal time.'

'No.' He smiled again and took a step towards the door. 'You rest. Have a slow morning and come in around ten.'

Rachael stood and faced him, her back to her mother and Declan. 'OK. I'll walk you to the car.'

'Will I see you tomorrow, Joe?' Declan was beside his mother in an instant.

Joe looked at his son and felt a pang of paternal love sweep through him. It was such a foreign emotion but one that felt so right, so instantly right. This time his smile was genuine. 'Sure. We'll arrange something after school.'

'Can we go to the movie set again?'

'Not tomorrow, but we'll think of something.' Something a little less stimulating, he added silently.

'Cool.' Then, to Joe's utter surprise, Declan gave him a hug. It was a male hug where only their torsos touched and he gave a few hearty slaps on Joe's back. 'Thanks, Dad.' The words were said softly but clearly, and for the second time in as many minutes Joe felt tears begin to prick behind his eyes

Rachael watched them closely, her throat constricting with love. She could see the surprise and struggle Joe was having because the emotions were too new for him to effectively hide them. When Declan released him, she said, 'Get your things together and help Grandma tidy up.'

'OK.' Declan beamed. 'See you tomorrow, Dad.'

Joe headed to the door and sucked in an urgent breath of air once he was outside. 'It's OK, Rach. You don't have to come out. It's getting cold.'

Rachael shut the front door behind her and headed across the grass. 'What happened, Joe?'

'What?' He stopped beside the car and turned to face her 'Another Spanish Inquisition?'

She smiled. 'It won't work because you're expecting it

Besides, you already know my secret forms of torture.' Joe returned her smile and the weight that had settled on her heart lifted. She reached out and took his hand in hers. 'Parenting isn't an easy thing to do but the only way to learn is by experiencing everything and making the best of it.'

'You don't think I'll stuff him up?'

'Oh, Joe. Is that what's bothering you?' Rachael shook her head and took a step closer. 'I wouldn't let you near Declan if I didn't trust you. Those three weeks we spent together were the happiest of my life. I can't find the words to describe how…magnificent and wondrous it was. We got to know each other on the most intimate of levels and I'm not just talking about our physical relationship.' She brushed her fingers through the hair at his temple. 'We touched souls, Joe. We may not have spilled every detail about our pasts but for who we were right at that moment in time, we bonded… And it's happening all over again.'

'Mmm.' Her touch was making him crazy and he felt as though he was beginning to drown once more, drown in the reality that was Rachael. Her words were true. The bond they shared had already survived so much, and in the back of his mind were the same doubts he'd had all those years ago. Could he make it work? Would he let her down?

He shoved the doubts aside…at least for the moment as he gathered her into his arms.

'You're an incredible man, Joseph Silvermark,' she whispered close to his ear.

'You've changed, Rach. I don't remember you being this forthright before.'

She chuckled and the vibrations from her body passed through to him. 'I'm stronger, Joe. Not necessarily in body, but definitely in mind…and soul.' She pressed a kiss to his neck before pulling back to look into his eyes. 'I'm also more determined to fight for what I want.'

He raised an eyebrow. 'Is that so?'

'I guess you could say I've matured.'

'A word I've always hated.'

'Because you were forced to mature way too fast.' She sighed and hugged him close again, loving the feel of their bodies together. 'Wisdom, Joe.' She pressed kisses to his neck, working her way around to his ear. 'Wisdom and peace come from knowing yourself better, and that's how I feel at the moment.' She nipped at his earlobe with her teeth and was rewarded with a groan. 'Like that, eh?' She did it again, chuckling when he groaned once more. 'I like it when you're at my mercy.'

'And I like being there.' Becoming impatient, he began his own onslaught and after pressing a few kisses to her exposed neck he worked his way around to her mouth. She allowed him one quick kiss before she pulled back and smiled at him.

'I think we can do better than that.'

'Really? I *know* we can.' She laughed, feeling young and free once more as his mouth found hers.

The kiss wasn't hot or hungry, it wasn't sweet and sensual, but more a kiss of…familiarity, and it reminded her just how familiar they'd been with each other in the past. He made her feel safe, comfortable and special. They had affected each other's lives in such dramatic ways and now they had the opportunity to discover new things.

His arms tightened around her as though he sensed her need. She was everything he remembered and more, and he knew he would never get tired of the feel of her mouth against his. They fitted perfectly together—always had—and now… now they were fitting perfectly once more.

He groaned as her mouth responded in complete synchronicity with his. She knew exactly how to get a response from him, both verbally and physically. He could feel the emotions between them spiral…spiral upwards towards the next level. They felt so right together and he couldn't deny it. She gave him hope and that was something he hadn't felt in an extremely long time.

The more he deepened the kiss, the more potent the emotions became. His lips were possessive on hers, staking a claim, and there was no way she would deny him. It felt as though he wanted to mark her, to let the world know she belonged to him, and although she'd always thought of herself as an emancipated woman, she was more than willing to forgo the label if it meant he stayed by her side.

The pressure continued to build, both of them clinging fiercely to each other as they eagerly took and gave in equal amounts. It was the way it had always been between them—equal—and even though she had this new inner strength, he couldn't help but be attracted to it. She was still *his* Rachael.

'Should I get excited about this?' Declan's voice floated over the front lawn towards them.

Rachael broke free and tried to step out of Joe's grasp to face her son, but Joe was taking his sweet time about releasing her.

'Declan.' She cleared her throat. 'Sorry, darling. I didn't hear you come out.'

'I'm not surprised.' He grinned like a Cheshire cat.

'You ready to go, honey?'

'Yes.'

She nodded and smoothed a hand down her trousers. 'OK. I'll be right there.' She turned. 'See you tomorrow, Joe.'

He grinned, obviously enjoying her discomfort. 'Yes, you will, but not before ten or I'll kick you out.'

She smiled. It was just like him to lighten the mood, to help her to feel less self-conscious. 'Are you sure about that? Lots of pregnant women and children are on my list.'

A smile touched his lips and his shrug was also a little self-conscious. 'I'll manage.'

And she knew he would. He always did. 'Thanks.' She squeezed his hand, unsure whether or not to kiss him goodbye. His smile widened and she realised he was once more reading her mind. Thankfully, he took the decision out of her hands by bending to kiss her lips, not once, not twice, but three times.

'Don't start again,' Declan called. 'It's freezing.'

Joe chuckled and released Rachael. ''Night, Declan.'

''Night, Joe.' Declan's grin was wide and teasing as she walked over to him. They both waited for Joe to drive away, waving as he did so.

'Let's get going. I've lost feeling in my toes and my eyelashes are starting freeze.'

'And whose fault is that?' They said goodbye to Elizabeth and drove back to the hotel. 'Are you and my dad getting back together?' Declan asked hopefully.

Rachael sighed and shook her head. 'I don't know, Dec. We're still attracted to each other...'

'That's a good thing, right?'

'But there's so much we need to sort out.'

'Do you still love him?'

'Declan.'

'No. Come on, Mum. Do you?'

'I've always loved Joe.'

'Yeah, but, you know, not in that abstract way but the real way.'

'Although I want to say I do, I'm also very confused. I'm sorry if that's not the answer you're looking for but it's all I can give you. Things have happened so fast but then...' she smiled '...they usually do between Joe and me.'

The phone beside Rachael's bed rang and she woke with a start, glancing at the clock as she picked up the receiver. Three o'clock in the morning usually meant bad news.

'Rach, it's Joe.'

'Joe? What's wrong? Are you all right?'

'I'm fine. Sorry to wake you but I thought you'd like to

know. I stopped in at the hospital to check on Wong. His surgery went well and he's finally in ICU, being monitored closely. Everyone's happy with the way the operations went but he still hasn't regained consciousness.'

'To be expected. And Rino?'

'Not a problem with him except his clavicle needed plating, not just strapping as Zac initially thought. The external fixator's on and I think Zac is fixing the right tib-fib fracture later today.'

'Good. Thanks for letting me know. I appreciate it.'

'How's Declan?'

She could hear the hesitancy in his voice. 'Snoring, actually.' She smiled as she listened to her son.

'No more nightmares?'

'No. He's out cold, which is good for him.'

'I'm glad. Well, I'd better let you get to sleep.'

'Is that what you're going to do, Joe? Sleep?'

'Soon.'

'Want to talk for a while?'

'And have you psychoanalyse me?'

She chuckled. 'I could always tell you what I'm wearing.' There was silence, and for a moment she thought he'd hung up. 'Joe?'

'Want to give me heart failure?' Her rich chuckle came down the line again and he groaned.

'Not particularly. I like your heart beating…close to mine.'

'Rachael.' He drawled her name slowly, a warning sign. 'I know which room you're staying in so be careful what you say.'

'I'm wearing…' she began seductively. 'A low-riding pair of…' Again she paused before finishing in her normal voice. 'Flannelette pyjamas.'

'If you think that's going to douse the flames, think again, sweetheart. You've now got me sitting here thinking of all the ways to get you out of those pyjamas.'

'Oh.' It was Rachael's turn to gasp.

'Yes, "*oh*". Don't play with fire, unless you plan to get burnt.' He paused. 'You and I were always hot stuff.'

'Mmm. I have a vivid memory.'

'So do I.' He paused and dragged in a deep breath. 'And now, my sweet Rachael, before this goes any further, I'm going to hang up the phone, go home and take a cold shower.'

'Doesn't sound like a bad idea. These pyjamas have become stifling.'

'Rachael.' Again the warning was there.

She laughed. 'I'll see you in the morning and thanks for the update.'

'Remember, I'll kick you out if you show up at the clinic any time before ten.'

Her smile intensified. 'I wouldn't dream of it.' She paused. 'Thanks, Joe.'

'For what?'

'For being you.'

CHAPTER EIGHT

RACHAEL did exactly as she'd been told the next morning, apart from the leisurely breakfast suggestion. They were up in time to get Declan to school, and afterwards she arranged to meet the estate agent at the apartment Declan and her parents had chosen. She liked what she saw, and as it suited her requirements she started the ball rolling—much to the delight of the estate agent.

She called the hospital and was told by the ICU sister that Wong still hadn't regained consciousness. The sister then transferred Rachael's call through to the coronary care unit so she could speak to Ethel, who was happy to report that Alwyn was being transferred from the unit down to the ward.

'That's wonderful news.'

'Your Dr Silvermark came around early this morning to see him. I wasn't here and Alwyn said it was before eight o'clock, but he said Dr Silvermark was very happy with his progress.'

'I'm glad. You remember to take care of yourself as well. When Alwyn is discharged, you'll need all your strength and patience to cope with him.'

Ethel laughed. 'You're right, dear. I know you are.' They chatted for a few more minutes before Rachael rang off, pleased to hear of Alwyn's progress.

By ten o'clock she'd managed to wander around the shops and buy herself a new pair of boots and was at the practice as promised. Helen smiled as she walked in the door.

'You look chipper.'

Rachael laughed. 'I don't think I've ever been called that before, but thank you.' She smiled politely at the patients in the waiting room and headed through to her office. Helen came in with her list. 'How's Joe this morning?'

Helen grinned. 'Up to his armpits in pregnant women—and I don't mean literally.'

'Thank goodness. Well, it was his idea I start late, but I hope it hasn't disrupted your schedule.'

'No, no. I'm glad you've had a relaxing morning.' Helen hesitated. 'You know, Joe doesn't usually do things like that.'

'What, giving his colleague a morning off?'

'No, I mean taking on a clinic full of expectant mothers and babies. They've never been his style and although he's a fantastic doctor, everyone has their sub-speciality. Family medicine isn't Joe's.'

'Perhaps the fact he's now a father makes a difference.'

Helen smiled again. 'That's exactly what I was thinking—that and the fact I think he's still smitten with you. He'd do anything for you.'

'Not smitten,' Rachael corrected quickly. 'Attracted but never smitten. Anyway, I'm here now so I'd better get my list under way.'

'OK.' Helen crossed to the door then turned. 'I don't want you to think I'm interfering but I've known Joe a long time and I just wanted to say that after his American…holiday, if you can call surfing a holiday. Anyway, when he finally returned, he was different. That's when he started getting real direction in his life and it took him quite a few years before he told me about you. The way he talked about you…' Helen sighed romantically. 'I've never heard him talk about anyone else that way before. You touched him, Rachael, and you touched him deeply. In Joe's world, that's a very rare thing to have happen.'

Rachael nodded. 'I understand. Thank you.' She'd always hoped she'd left a lasting impression on Joe and not just one of lust. Hearing this from Helen, a woman he trusted, made her able to believe what she and Joe had felt for each other back then had indeed been the real thing. Now she had a better understanding of the man, she could see why he had backed away.

It brought a lot of 'what-ifs' to her mind, and as she wasn't the type of person to indulge in what-ifs, she forced herself to concentrate on her work. She contacted the hospital and received a positive update on Grace, glad to hear she hadn't had another seizure during the night and was booked to have further tests later today. The neurology registrar seemed extremely confident and Rachael was glad Grace was being looked after by such a person.

Next, she headed to the waiting room and called her first patient through. Starting work at ten o'clock meant lunchtime came around very quickly, but it was after one o'clock before Rachael ventured into the kitchen to make a cup of coffee.

'Hi.' Joe's voice washed over her as he walked into the room. 'What a morning!'

Rachael smiled. 'How did it go?'

He nodded slowly. 'Not bad, if I do say so myself. I think some of the women were a bit surprised to be seeing me, but I managed.' He paused, then smiled. 'There are some really cute kids in the world.'

Rachael couldn't help but laugh.

'What?'

'Nothing. Hey, any news on Wong? I called the hospital this morning but they said no change.'

Joe shook his head. 'No change.'

'I'm sorry.'

His answer was a heavy shrug.

'Coffee?' It seemed so lame to offer something so mundane when his friend was so sick.

'Thanks.' Then he paused. 'Got any plans for lunch?'

'Actually, I hadn't thought that far.' She glanced pointedly at her watch. 'Besides, my afternoon clinic starts in twenty minutes.'

With that, Joe put her coffee cup on the bench and took her hand, dragging her out of the room. 'Where are we going?'

'Back soon,' he said to Helen as they barrelled out the door and headed down the street to a small café.

'Joe?'

'Lunch, Rach. You need to eat.' He didn't let go of her hand until she was seated at a table with a menu in front of her.

'Is this your idea of a date? If so, your dating skills need brushing up.'

'What do you want? They're pretty fast here, but only if you don't take all day to order.'

'Be still, my beating heart.' She glanced at the menu. 'Club sandwich.'

'Excellent.' The waitress came over. 'Two coffees and two club sandwiches, please.' He smiled at the other woman as she wrote down their orders, and Rachael watched as the waitress melted. She was sure he knew the power of his smile and used it whenever it suited him. He'd probably used it on every one of the women he'd seen this morning and had had them walking out saying how wonderful that sweet Dr Silvermark was.

When the waitress had gone, Joe looked across at Rachael. 'So how was your morning? Did you enjoy a long, leisurely breakfast?'

'No. No time. I did, however,' she quickly continued, 'speak to the real estate agent about the apartment Declan liked.'

He raised his eyebrows. 'So you'll be moving soon?'

'Hopefully some time next week.'

'Terrific.' He paused, then leaned forward a little. 'Tell me what you bought this morning.'

'What makes you think I bought something?'

He laughed. 'When you were eighteen years old, you certainly knew how to shop. Still have your shoe fetish?'

'What woman doesn't?'

'Exactly. So what did you buy?'

Rachael shook her head. 'I shouldn't be amazed you know me so well,' she mumbled, and he chuckled. 'Boots. OK? I bought a pair of boots.'

'Flats or heels?'

'Flats.' She smiled.

'Leather or suede?'

Her smile increased. 'Leather.'

'Black or…' He thought for a moment. 'Red?'

She laughed. 'I love it when you talk shopping. Black, but the red ones looked good, too.'

'I don't even want to ask how much they cost.'

'They'll last me a long time.'

'That means they were expensive.'

'How do you know?'

He raised his eyebrows and grinned like the cat who'd got the cream. 'I know you. Remember?'

'Don't you find it amazing just how much information we've retained about each other?'

He sobered instantly. 'No.'

They sat there looking at each other, absorbing each other. It was as though, for that moment, only the two of them existed. It wasn't the first time it had happened and it wouldn't be the last.

One of the waitresses dropped something, startling Rachael and breaking the bond. She sat up straighter in her chair, feeling a little self-conscious just sitting there staring at Joe in the middle of a coffee shop. Then again, he'd been staring back at her.

'What are you going to do at the end of next week?'

'Hopefully, move into my new apartment.'

'I don't mean that. I mean about work.'

'Oh. Work.' She paused. 'Why?'

'I'm having the papers drawn up to make you a permanent doctor in the clinic.'

'What?'

'I'm offering you a partnership.'

Rachael was speechless. She sat and stared at Joe as though he'd just grown another head. 'What?' she finally managed again. 'Joe, you can't just do that.' She frowned at him. How dared he do this to her? Just when she'd started to relax and feel as though she had some control over her life, he sprang this on her.

'Why not? I own the practice.'

'What about Alison? She leaves to have a baby and you penalise her by giving her job, permanently, to someone else.'

'Alison is more than welcome to come back once she's finished maternity leave. She doesn't want to be a partner in a practice, especially now she's starting her family, and she only wants to work part time so, you see, there is more than enough room for you.'

'And what if I want to have more children and work part time? What then?' She'd meant her words to stun him and she wasn't disappointed. Colour began to drain from his face and he clenched his jaw.

'Is that what you want? I thought you were past all that.'

'Why? Because Declan's a teenager?' Rachael folded her arms across her chest once more.

'There'd be a very large gap in their ages.'

'Obviously, and there's nothing I can do to change that. Still, I believe you at least need to consider that before you offer me a partnership.'

'Do you expect me to put conditions on it?'

'Well, if I were to get pregnant and wanted to work part time, I wouldn't want you to accuse me of not holding up my end of the agreement.' The waitress brought their food and this time Joe had no melting smiles to dish out. Instead, h sat there and glared at Rachael. 'Besides,' she continued as she reached for the sugar, 'partnerships cost money, and I don't think I'm quite ready to invest in one right now.' She smiled politely at him as she stirred her coffee.

'Who are you going to have these children with?'

She took a sip of her drink. 'I beg your pardon? I don't believe you—as my employer—have any right to be discussing my private life.'

'Rachael.' He growled her name and leaned a little closer. 'Declan is my son.'

'Yes, he's mine, too. We established all this a few days ago. Remember?'

'You're being facetious.'

'Yes, I am. My point is, I think you need to give your idea a little more thought.'

'You don't want to work with me,' he stated with a scowl. He glanced at her, then looked away. He was angry but beneath that anger she'd seen the pain.

'I never said that. OK. You tell me why you want me there.'

'You're a good doctor.'

'So is Alison. Come on, Joe, what's your main motivation here? If it's Declan, I won't restrict access to him just because I'm not working with you.'

She waited but all he did was to cross his arms over his chest and scowl at her.

'Joe, I'm not rejecting *you*. I'm saying I don't think you've thought this idea through thoroughly enough. I don't know whether or not I'm going to have more children. I have enough to concentrate on at the moment with Declan, his schooling and moving into an apartment, but I also don't know what the future will bring.' She put her hand on the table, waiting for him to put his into it.

He stirred sugar into his coffee, picked up the cup, took a

long sip and glanced down at her hand—rejecting it. Rachael didn't budge.

'Come on. Take my hand and let's be friends.'

'What if I don't want to be friends?'

She couldn't help but laugh.

'What? Now you're laughing at me.' His tone was incredulous.

'No. Oh, Joe. You sounded just like Declan. I'm still getting used to all the similarities and it's strange to hear his pouting, whiny voice from you.'

'I was not pouting neither was I whining.' He slapped his hand into hers as though to prove his point.

She smiled. 'Joe, let's just take things a little slower.'

'Will you at least agree to stay on until the end of the month?' His thumb began to make little circles on her hand, and with each sweeping movement it felt as though a charge was shooting up her arm and exploding throughout her body.

Rachael tried to quash the emotions and think. It was almost impossible. Now that she and Joe had established a rapport, it might be good to stay on for a bit longer. It would give Joe a chance to really cement his relationship with Declan so when she eventually did move to another practice, Joe wouldn't feel too self-conscious about spending time with his son and not having Rachael there as a fall-back plan.

Then again, she had to take her emotions for Joe into account. Sure, it might be in Declan's best interests if she stayed for a bit longer, but what about hers? If she was honest with herself, she'd admit that Joe was far too special to her. History was repeating itself and where history had ended badly last time, it didn't give her much hope for a happy ending this time.

She frowned. 'I need to think about it, Joe.'

'Come on, Rach. Can't you give me an answer? You either will or you won't.'

'It's not that simple.'

'Yes, it is. It's a job.'

'A job that can have a lot of repercussions. I've never been a spontaneous person, Joe.'

'You married me.'

'That was different and you know it. I've never done things on the spur of the moment—apart from that.' And look how it turned out, she wanted to say. Recovering from a broken heart, feeling used and worthless and then discovering you were pregnant was not a good recommendation for her to spend more time with Joe, especially when it appeared she was more than willing to repeat past mistakes.

He let go of her hand. 'How much time? I need to know so I can arrange another locum.' He was all business now, his emotions hidden behind his professional mask.

'You'll have an answer by the end of the day.'

'Thank you.' He turned and motioned to the waitress, who quickly came over. 'We need this to go so would you mind wrapping them up for us, please?' The waitress took their plates. 'Drink your coffee,' he muttered, and followed his own advice.

The atmosphere as they walked back to the practice was the opposite of when they'd walked to the café. Joe's stride was brisk and determined and Rachael didn't even bother to try and keep up. When he realised he was outstripping her, he slowed down a little but only out of politeness, she was sure.

She refused to feel any guilt over his mood. As they walked into the practice, Joe merely nodded at Helen before disappearing into his consulting room.

'Problem?' Helen asked.

'Didn't get his own way.'

'Ah. The partnership. You turned him down?'

'You knew?'

'He asked me to get his solicitor on the line and I guessed.' She opened her mouth to say something else but closed it.

'Go on. What were you going to add?'

'Nothing.'

'Helen.'

The other woman shook her head and the clinic door opened, bringing her first patient for the afternoon. It was Tracy Rainer and her son. This time she didn't have Bobby in the pram but instead she was wearing a sling, Bobby sleeping soundly against her. They could just see the top of his downy head.

'Hi.' Rachael greeted Tracy warmly. 'Come right through, Tracy.' Rachael handed Helen the bag containing the sandwich. 'Would you mind putting that in the fridge for me, please?' Without waiting for an answer, she collected Tracy's file and headed down to her consulting room.

At least today Tracy looked a little more relaxed than she had on Monday, and Bobby appeared more settled.

'How are you feeling?'

'Like a person again.' Tracy smiled. 'This sling is fantastic—once I figured out how to put it on, that is. I can't believe how different I feel.'

'I take it you've managed to get some sleep.'

'Yes. On Monday night I brought the cot into the bedroom, fed him upright and gave him the antacid like you said, and he slept for four hours! I was waking up every hour to check he was all right because it was so unlike him.'

Rachael smiled. 'I can quite understand it. And last night?'

'Again, he slept for four hours after the feed and I did the same.'

'Well done.'

'The antacid has helped him so much and now that I know to keep him upright so he doesn't get reflux, he's more settled.'

Rachael sat at her desk and made a note of these changes in the casenotes. 'And your mother-in-law?'

Tracy grimaced. 'I was reluctant to call her, especially after

Bobby had slept on Monday night, but I decided that you knew best and so I did it.'

'Good. And?' Rachael prompted eagerly.

'It wasn't as bad as I'd thought it would be. I think you were right. She wanted to help and I wasn't letting her, so she just criticised me instead. Anyway, she had Bobby for two hours yesterday at my house and then today I dropped him at her place and went shopping.'

'Well done! I am so proud of you.' Rachael beamed. 'I hope you spent some money on yourself.'

'I did…and I bought a few things for Bobby.'

'Naturally.'

'And I bought this.' Tracy reached inside her bag and brought out a little square parcel. She smiled shyly as she held it out to Rachael.

'For me?' Rachael was stunned. 'Thank you.' With great surprise, she unwrapped it to find a lovely photo frame inside. 'Thank you,' she said again. 'It's lovely. I'm moving into a new apartment soon so this will be a lovely addition to our new home.'

'Are you moving in with Dr Silvermark?'

Rachael blinked with astonishment. 'No. Why do you ask?'

'Oh. Sorry.' Tracy shrugged. 'It's just that your son looks just like him and I thought, you know, with you working here and…' Tracy waved her words away. 'Forget it.'

'Joe is Declan's father and…it's a long story.' She stood up and smiled at the sleeping baby. 'I'm reluctant to wake him when he's sleeping so soundly.' She peeked into the sling and brushed a kiss across his head. 'Make an appointment for next week and I'll review his reflux then. Don't change the dosage of antacid as it seems to be working, but if things change and you want me to see him, bring him in earlier.'

'OK.' Tracy smiled and Rachael was glad to have helped her. 'I'll see you next week.'

After they'd left, Rachael wrote up her notes and smiled as she put the photo frame away, still touched by the gesture.

When her last patient had left and she'd written up the notes, she headed into the kitchen, surprised Declan wasn't around. His schoolbag was in the corner so at least she knew he wasn't too far away. 'Probably talking to Joe,' she muttered, as she pulled her sandwich from the refrigerator and turned the kettle on. Sitting at the table, she unwrapped the slightly soggy club sandwich and bit into it gratefully.

Three mouthfuls later, Joe came into the kitchen. 'What! You're just eating lunch now?'

Rachael shrugged. 'You know what it's like, Joe. There was no time before.'

'I found time.'

'Yes, but you eat faster than I do. It's no big deal. Don't freak out.'

'Freak out?'

'Declan's favourite phrase.' She took another bite.

'What's my favourite phrase?' Declan asked, coming into the kitchen.

'Freak out,' Joe said.

'Yeah.' He grinned sheepishly. 'I guess I do say it a bit Why? Who's freaking out?'

'Your father,' Rachael said, after swallowing her mouthful

'Your mother's just eating her lunch now.'

'I can see that. Why does that freak you out?'

'Because it's not lunchtime.'

'Oh.' Declan frowned then shrugged. 'Taste good?'

'Terrific,' she said with her mouth half-full.

Declan shrugged again. 'What's the problem? She's a doctor. I thought all doctors ate at odd hours.'

Rachael swallowed her last mouthful. 'That was delicious Kettle boiled? I'm ready for a cup of coffee.' She threw he rubbish in the bin and washed her hands. 'Dec? You want drink?'

'No, thanks.'

'Joe?'

He shook his head. 'I'm going to take Declan down to the golf range.'

'Now?' Rachael glanced at her watch. 'It's after five.'

'We're not going to play a round, just have a few practice shots.'

Rachael raised her eyebrows. '*You* play golf?'

'Yeah. So?'

'You. You play golf.'

'Why do you keep saying that? Yes, I play golf. What's the big deal?'

Rachael couldn't help the chuckle that escaped her lips but she quickly squashed it when he frowned. 'Sorry. It…it just doesn't seem like your type of game. You know, being out with nature—trees, grass. Hitting a little white ball around.'

'So what *is* my type of game?'

'I don't know. Ice hockey?'

'Ice hockey?'

'Cool,' Declan said.

'It's a more physical sport, more smash 'em up and stuff.' Rachael made her coffee and took a sip. 'But I guess I'm still thinking of the Joe of the past. So, what time can I expect you back at the hotel?'

'Around seven.' Joe headed for the door. 'In time for dinner. You can wear your new boots!'

He raised his eyebrows teasingly before walking out, but stopped in the corridor when he heard Declan say to Rachael, 'A family dinner. Cool.'

The word *family* caused an icy chill to sweep over his body. Is that what they were becoming? A family? Was that what Declan wanted? A mother and a father? Together? Although he was attracted to Rachael, he wasn't sure he was cut out to play happy families.

'Don't get too excited,' Rachael added. 'It's just dinner.'

'Are you sure that's all? I think he's interested in a lot more than that.'

'Declan!' Rachael could feel her cheeks flush with embarrassment. 'Shh.'

'What? Have you forgotten I caught you two playing tonsil hockey last night? He likes you, Mum.'

'So? There's more to Joe than meets the eye, Dec, and I don't mean that in a bad way. I think he wants to be part of your life and that's great, but happy families just isn't Joe's style.'

'What about you, Mum? Do you want to play happy families with Joe?' Declan wriggled his eyebrows suggestively and Rachael momentarily covered her face. 'You love him, don't you.'

'I gave you my answer last night.'

'I want a different answer.'

Rachael hesitated, unsure whether to confide in her son. What if the truth hurt him? What if she got them both hurt? She dropped her hands and looked at him. He was watching her, his blue gaze intense, and she realised he already knew the answer. She shrugged and spoke with the utmost sincerity.

'I love Joe. I always have and I always will. He's the only man for me, but I've also learned to accept him for who he is, Dec. Spending time with you, getting to know you—if that's all he's capable of, then that's what I accept. You're my first priority and I think you'll soon become his. That's enough for me.'

Declan crossed the room to hug his mother. 'I love you, Mum, even though I think you're lying to yourself.'

Rachael laughed. 'Probably. Get going. Joe's waiting for you. Leave your schoolbag. I'll take it.'

Joe, still standing outside the room, quickly walked down to his consulting room, desperate to pull himself together. Rachael loved him? Was that true? Was she just saying that for Declan's benefit? And what sort of love was it? Was it a friendship love? A compassionate love or the real thing? The emotions he felt for her were increasing every moment he spent with her and they were scaring him senseless…just as they had all those years before.

When Declan appeared in his doorway, Joe shoved the thoughts aside. 'Just let me tidy up here and then we can go.' He shuffled some papers around on his desk, checked his pocket for his car keys and headed to tell Helen they were leaving.

'Have fun, boys,' she called.

'Boys?' Declan asked as they walked to Joe's car.

'She still sees me as a wayward teenager.' Joe's words were light but filled with humour. 'I guess she always will.'

They both climbed into the car and put their seat belts on. 'Were you a wayward teenager?'

Joe tensed. 'Kind of.'

'So what did you do way back then?'

Joe relaxed and smiled. 'You mean when dinosaurs walked the earth?' He started the engine and pulled out onto the street.

'Yeah.'

'Why do you want to know?'

'What do you mean?'

'Why? Has your mum said something?'

'No. I want to know because you're my dad. I know all about Mum because I've lived with her and seen the photo albums and heard Grandma and Grandad talk, but with you…' Declan shrugged. 'I just have blanks.'

'What did your mum tell you about me?'

'While I was growing up?'

'Yeah.' Joe gripped the steering wheel.

'She said my dad was a handsome man who always made her laugh and who she loved very much. She said you needed to find out who you were. I never really understood that but whenever I asked her if you loved me, she said she was sure you did.'

Joe found it difficult to swallow the lump in his throat. Rachael had had every reason in the world to put him down, to tell her son how badly his father had treated her. The disgust and revulsion he felt about the day they'd had their marriage annulled swamped him.

'Until I met you the other day, Mum and I hadn't talked about you in years.'

Joe nodded slowly, clenching his teeth. 'I didn't know about you. If I had…' He trailed off. What would he have done? Honestly? He didn't have a clue. The fact that the situation had been forced upon him now was different, but if Rachael had managed to find him all those years ago when she'd first discovered she was pregnant, what would he have done?

He'd have walked away.

'We were different people back then. Your mother and I.'

'You were young. I can't believe Mum was only eighteen when she had me. She sometimes says we've grown up together.'

'She's a lot stronger than she used to be. I admire that.'

'What else do you like about her?'

If Joe hadn't overheard the conversation Declan had just had with his mother, he probably wouldn't have been as nervous. 'Lots of things.'

'Like what, specifically?'

Joe pulled into the car park of the golf range and turned the engine off. The silence engulfed them and when he spoke, even he heard the deep emotion in his words. 'I like her hair. Every time I've seen a woman with jet-black hair, it's always reminded me of her.'

'Do you still love her?'

Joe turned and looked at his son and realised that, regardless of what turmoil he was going through, he owed Declan nothing less than the truth. 'I don't know. I think on some level I will always love her. She's one in a million but…'

'But you're not into happy families.' Declan shrugged with feigned nonchalance and it was a mannerism Joe recognised as one of his own. 'It's cool,' the boy said, and pointed to the range. 'Let's go.' He opened the door and climbed out.

As Joe watched him walk away, he realised his son was nowhere near as adept at hiding his true feelings as he himself was…and he envied the kid.

CHAPTER NINE

RACHAEL returned to the hotel where she showered and dressed in a pair of jeans and a pale pink top. She'd just finished drying her hair when the door opened and male voices intruded into her solitude.

'Mum. The driving range was awesome. I was whacking those little white balls everywhere, wasn't I, Dad?' He glanced momentarily at his father before continuing. 'At first I had some trouble but then Dad showed me what I was doing wrong and then I got it on the next try. Didn't I, Dad?'

'You did.'

'I take it you had fun.' Rachael laughed and put her arm around his waist.

'No, it was boring. Whaddya think?' He broke away. 'I'm gonna change.' He grabbed some clothes and headed to the bathroom. Rachael sighed with relief when he'd disappeared. Her son was happy. That was all that mattered in life. 'It stinks all girly in here,' he grumbled through the door, and both she and Joe laughed.

'Thanks, Joe.'

Joe shrugged. 'For what?'

'For making him happy.'

'Hopefully, his mind's not too stimulated and he'll be able to sleep tonight. How does he do it? Survive on such a small amount of sleep?'

'The past few days will catch up with him.'

'When?'

'On the weekend. Trust me. You'll hardly see him on Saturday and Sunday and if you do, it will be after midday before he surfaces. He sleeps and he sleeps and he sleeps, and there's no way I interrupt that.'

'Fair enough.' Joe walked over to the window and looked out. Rachael felt the atmosphere in the room change. She waited, knowing he wanted to say something. It irritated her that she knew him so well, and at the same time she drew comfort from the same fact.

'Rach.'

'Yes.'

'Are you staying on until the end of the month?'

'Yes.'

He turned to face her. 'Really?'

Rachael sighed, knowing she was in for heartache, but whether she stayed or not, the pain would come. 'Yes.'

'Why?'

'Pardon?'

'Why?'

'Because it's good for the patients, good for Declan and gives me time to get my apartment established before looking around for another job.'

'That's it?'

She shrugged. 'What else is there? You asked and I've given you my answer.'

Joe turned back to the window. Why wouldn't she tell him? He'd overheard her telling Declan she loved him.

He stared at his reflection in the window. What had you expected, Silvermark? He shook his head. Did you honestly expect her to come right out and say she's staying on because she loves you? Rachael wasn't the sort of person to let her heart get in the way of her judgement—at least not now. Could he blame her? Fifteen years ago he'd taken the love he'd offered so selflessly and had thrown it back at her. No, he'd trampled on it and *then* rejected it. He'd been scared, confused and had let his defences wreck the best thing that had ever happened to him—receiving an honest love from an honest woman.

Joe shifted so he could see her reflection in the window. She was just standing there, hands in the pockets of her jeans, the pink top making her eyes more vibrant and her black hair shine beautifully as it hung loose around her shoulders.

He turned to face her and she saw the desire in his eyes. She also saw total confusion and her heart went out to him. Joe wasn't the sort of man who was easy with emotions, and although he'd come a long way, he still had much more to experience. If she took a step in faith, if she guided him through the rocky terrain, then maybe…just maybe…there might be a future for all three of them. She stood her ground, knowing this time Joe needed to take the first step. She could help him, she was willing to help him, but he had to be ready to receive the help. She dug her hands further into her pockets.

Joe wished she'd cross the room and put her arms around his neck. Then he'd be back in control because he knew exactly what to do when Rachael's body was pressed against his. She didn't move. Although he saw need and desire in her eyes, he realised she wasn't going to do the chasing. She'd just stand there and wait for him. If he went to her, she'd welcome him with open arms—of that he was certain. If he didn't, she'd stand there, pick up the pieces of her life and move on. The thought terrified him.

'OK.' Declan came out the bathroom and Rachael instantly broke eye contact with Joe and turned to face her son. 'I'm starving.' He threw his school clothes onto her bed and Rachael immediately straightened them out.

'Where do you want to go?'

'Dad and I saw this great Mexican restaurant so we thought we'd go there. It's only a block down the road so we can walk.' Declan shrugged into his jacket.

'Sounds good. Let's go.' Rachael pulled on her new boots.

'Nice.' Joe nodded.

She smiled, thrilled with his comment, and shrugged into her jacket. Joe walked through the door Declan held open. 'Have you got the key-card?' Rachael checked before the door shut behind them.

'Yes, Mum,' Declan declared in a bored tone. 'Here's mine.' Declan waved it in front of her before handing it over. She slid it into her wallet then closed her bag. They rode the lift down and as they walked along the street, Rachael was a little startled to find Joe slipping his hand into hers. Not that she minded—quite the contrary—but it was so unexpected. She smiled up at him and gave his hand a squeeze before continuing her conversation with Declan about his school day.

'You see, Joe,' she said after they'd eaten their fill of the delicious Mexican food and were waiting for their dessert, 'the trick with kids is you have to ask them specific questions. "How was your day?" is only going to get you a general answer like, "Good".'

'What she's trying to say is that she's an expert at being nosy,' Declan added.

Rachael laughed good-naturedly. 'That's a mother's prerogative—nosy and nagging.'

'And you're the best at both, Mum.' Declan grinned at her. 'Every day I get bombarded with questions, especially as I've just started at a new school.'

'Well, what do you expect? I'm still learning all the players.'

'Players?' Joe frowned.

'Other students, teachers, that sort of thing.' Declan shrugged and Joe noticed the nonchalance. Don't get too close, the message said, but Rachael *was* close. She'd worked through Declan's defences and she knew her son well. It was evident in the way they interacted. Now she was working her way through his defences...and doing a good job of it.

'So...Declan.' Joe took a breath, realising Rachael wasn't

just making idle conversation but actually giving him parenting pointers. 'Who do you sit next to in maths?'

Rachael grinned.

'Oh, man. You're gonna start in on this, too?'

'How am I supposed to get to know you?' Joe leaned his elbows on the table. 'You're my son and we have years of catching up to do.' To his surprise, he noticed tears well in Declan's eyes.

'Does this mean you…want to be part of my life?'

Rachael held her breath, waiting anxiously for Joe's answer.

'Yes. In fact, I spoke to my solicitor today. I've had my will adjusted.'

'*What?*' Rachael and Declan spoke together, staring at him in stunned silence.

'It's my way of saying this is for life. You're my son, Declan. Nothing in the world is going to change that. It's important for me not only to find out about the past fourteen years of your life but to ensure your future is secure as well.'

'Joe.' It was on the tip of Rachael's tongue to tell him she was financially secure. That Declan was well taken care of, not only from herself but from her parents as well, but she closed her mouth, realising the enormity of what Joe had done. He was taking a chance. He was letting Declan in close, and had made it official by changing his will.

'That didn't come out right.' Joe raked a hand through his hair and Rachael's heart went out to him. 'I want to be there for you, son. I want to be your father. I'm just not sure I know how.'

Declan surprised them both by laughing as he brushed a few tears from his eyes. 'Are you kidding? You're the coolest guy I've ever met, and you're my *dad*! It's just so awesome.' He sobered a little. 'Mum's brill and she knows that, but there are…things—you know, guy stuff—and Mum doesn't have a clue. No offence, Mum.'

Rachael smiled. 'None taken. I'm glad you have Joe.'

'Don't get sappy on me, Mum.' Declan had himself under control once more but she knew it would take ages for the happy, silly grin to be wiped off his face. As far as Declan was concerned, all his Christmases *had* come at once.

Rachael still felt Joe watching her closely as she ate as much of her dessert as she could. Halfway through, she passed the rest to Declan who cleaned it up without a problem.

'Hey. How come he gets the leftovers?' Joe demanded.

'Looks as though you've got competition, Dec.'

Their conversation was easy, friendly and jovial as they finished up and walked…or rather *rolled* back to the hotel. 'I can't believe how much I ate.' Rachael patted her stomach. 'Well, here we are.' They stopped outside the entrance to the hotel.

'I'll ride up with you,' was all he said. Outside their door, Joe turned to Declan. 'Would you mind if I spoke to your mum alone for a minute?'

'Nah. I'll go start on my homework.'

'Have a shower first,' Rachael instructed, handing over the key-card.

'Yes, Mum,' he answered in the dull, boyish way he'd done for years. 'Nag, nag, nag.' He unlocked the room and held the door open.

'You may as well come in. Declan will be in the shower so we can talk.'

'Talk about me?' Declan was all ears.

'Yes. That's what parents do. Now go.'

She waited until the water was running then just as Joe was about to open his mouth, she held up her hand to stop him. Walking quietly over to the bathroom door, she banged loudly on it and received a yell from her son.

'Stop pressing your ear against the door and get in the shower. You're wasting water.'

Joe shook his head in amazement. 'How did you know?'

'He's a teenager and we're going to talk about him. Do you need more deductive reasoning than that?'

'Actually, I wanted to talk about you.' As usual, Joe paced the room then stopped and looked at her. It was his way of getting his thoughts together and she waited.

'OK. What do you want to know?'

'Tell me more about when you tried to find me.'

'OK.' She took a breath. 'Well, I tried when I discovered I was pregnant. When I couldn't track you down, I wondered whether you were dead. For years I didn't know but I forced myself to get on with my life. You'd rejected me and I had to live with that, so I did. Then, when Declan was about nine, you and I were both at the same medical conference.'

'What? Where?'

'It was a GP conference in Sydney.'

'You were there? Why didn't you say something?'

'Our paths didn't cross. I'd missed the first day of the conference because Declan hadn't been well on the flight to Sydney. My parents had flown in to look after him while I was at the conference and had a problem with their hotel reservation. I saw your name on the conference programme and couldn't believe it was really you, so I did some checking. Was there another Joseph Silvermark in the world? Were you associated with the conference? Did the hotel have a contact number for you? No one could give me any personal information as it was against conference and hotel policy, but at least I'd discovered you were not only alive but a doctor! I was stunned to discover you'd gone into medicine and proud at the same time. That probably sounds silly.'

'No. Go on,' he urged.

Rachael laced her fingers together and met his gaze. 'At the end of the second day, I saw you. It was late in the day and you were about to get into a taxi outside the hotel. I was in the lobby. You were with…a woman.'

Joe frowned as he thought back. 'Blonde?'

'Yes. She had her arms around your waist and you had your arm around her shoulders. You were smiling down at her and…' She shrugged. 'I couldn't do it.'

'Do what?'

'Go to you. Talk to you. Walk right up, ask if you even remembered me and then somehow figure out a way to tell you that you had a son! Especially when you had another woman hanging on your arm.'

'How could you think I wouldn't remember you?'

'I don't know.' She threw up her hands in despair. 'It all happened so fast. The two of you got into the taxi and it drove away. I hardly slept that night and was a nervous wreck the next day as I looked for you again.'

'I only stayed for the first two days.'

'So I found out.' She shrugged. 'That's when I started obsessing. Should I find you? Should I leave it? You'd never been keen on children so chances were you might even reject Declan. Still, you had a right to know and so I made some enquiries to see if there was some way I could find you. The Australian GPs' register at least told me where you'd been working, but when I contacted the practice, they told me you'd left for overseas and as you were a locum they had no way of contacting you.'

Joe shook his head in disbelief. 'That's when I started getting into the movie scene as an on-site medic. I was in America for a year then came back here and started up my practice.' He pushed his fingers through his hair. 'Wherever worked, I always gave them as few personal details as possible. Immediate contact numbers, address, that was it. It stemmed from my childhood of never giving out information that wasn't necessary.'

'It's OK, Joe. In a way it was good for me because at the time I was still clinging to a teenage girl's fantasy that we would one day get back together. Seeing you…' She stopped, unable to believe her voice had choked up.

'Seeing me with that girl? Why should that matter?'

'Why?' She couldn't believe how fast the tears sprang into her eyes. Her throat felt thick but she managed to get the words out. 'Joe, I loved you. You may have treated me like dirt, broken my heart and destroyed my self-worth when you ended our marriage—'

'Care to heap any more guilt on me?'

'I'm just stating the facts. Regardless of what had happened between us, you were Declan's father and the man I loved. I may not have *liked* you very much at times, but I've always loved you.'

'And now?' He took a step closer, trying to ignore the loud pounding of his heart. 'Do you love me now?'

She tilted her head to the side, a small, sincere smile on her lips. 'You know I do.'

Her words were matter-of-fact but he needed more. He needed to dig a little deeper. 'No. I don't mean love me as Declan's father but love *me*, accept *me*…as a man.'

'I know what you mean, Joe.' She took a breath and knew it was now or never. She'd laid herself, her heart, her pride on the line before, and now it was time to do it again. She'd told him she was strong, she'd told him she'd changed, ye right now she felt eighteen years old again. Young, excited unsure, thrilled. They were now almost toe to toe and he reached out to tenderly caress her cheek.

'Rach?'

She looked up at him, still smiling. A warmth sprea through him and he cupped her face in his hands.

'I love you, Joe.' The whispered words were said wit meaning and without hesitation. 'I always have and I alway will.'

With a smothered groan he pressed his mouth to her greedily taking everything she was willing to give. He realise in that second that he'd never be able to get enough of he She was like a drug and he was totally addicted.

Hot, powerful. Hungry, masterful. He had the ability to take her up so high and he was doing it right now. Lacing her fingers through his hair, she made sure his mouth stayed where it belonged as she continued to declare her love for him through her actions.

'Sweetheart,' he panted, when at last he pulled his mouth from hers. 'You make me crazy.' He pressed feathery-light kisses to her forehead and cheeks. 'No other woman affects me the way you do.'

'Not even the blonde?'

'Blonde? What blonde?'

'At the conference.' It hurt but she needed to know.

Joe leaned back, looking deeply into her eyes. 'Jealous?'

She lifted her chin in that defiant way he loved. 'Yes.' There was no point denying it. The thought of him with any other woman had always driven her insane.

'You have no reason to be. She's my half-sister.'

'Your…your sister?' Her words held a hint of disbelief.

'Half-sister. Her name's Melina, she lives in Sydney and is a bodyguard.'

'A bodyguard?'

'She grew up on the streets, remember. I had to teach her how to protect herself.' He shrugged and then settled his arms about her. 'The rest just followed.'

'Your sister.' Rachael shook her head.

'Yes.'

'She was your sister! I feel so stupid.'

'Rach.' He kissed her. 'Don't beat yourself up. You weren't to know. I didn't know you were there. You tried to find me and couldn't. It's all in the past.'

'Yes. But we need to sort through it, Joe. If we're going to have any hope for a future, we need to sort through the past.'

Any hope for a future… Any hope for a future. The words started repeating in his head and he could feel himself drawing

away, distancing himself mentally before he physically released his hold on her. She was still talking and he tried to
listen but he couldn't. *Any hope for a future…* Was that what
he wanted? A future with Rachael and Declan? He'd made
the decision to include Declan in his life but Rachael…he
hadn't been able to sort things through yet. He needed time.
Space. He took another step back and watched as she stopped
speaking, the blue of her eyes changing from warm and in-
viting to cold and protective.

'Joe?'

He swallowed and was disgusted to find his throat dry, his
heart pounding and his hands sweating. He wiped them down
his jeans.

Rachael folded her arms over her chest. 'Still pulling away?
Still unable to let go of your emotions and follow your heart?'

'Rachael—'

'No. I think it's time for some hard questions, Joe. You've
asked me so now I'm going to ask you. Do you love me?'

'Rach.'

'Answer the question, Joe. Do you love me? And I don'
mean in an old-friend way or even because I'm Declan'
mother. I'm talking about the love shared between a husband
and wife, between soul mates. The truest love you could
imagine…the love you once made me believe you felt. Is it
still there?'

He shrugged, feeling caged, trapped. 'I don't know.'

'Why not?'

'I don't know if I'm capable of love.'

'Do you love Declan?'

'That's different.'

'Do you love Helen?'

'Different.'

'Your sister?'

'Rachael.'

'No, Joe. You are capable of loving. I've seen it. I've *felt* it.'

'I'm not good with emotions.'

'Love isn't an emotion, Joe. Love triggers emotions. Safety, security, happiness. Pain, humiliation, hurt. Frustration, annoyance and anger, Joe. Right now, that's how I'm feeling. You are strong enough to love and your apathy drives me insane. I know you're capable because you loved me. You shared your heart with me, Joe, and for those amazing forty-eight hours you weren't afraid. You weren't on guard. You were alive. For the first time in your life you were alive, and it scared you. You were scared to feel, just as you are now.'

To her utter dismay, Rachael felt tears begin to slide down her cheeks. She sniffed. 'It's all too much,' she said to herself more than to him. 'The past few days have been too emotional. I think we need some time apart. Helen promised I would hardly see you, but you're there every time I turn around.' She pulled a tissue from her pocket as the tears refused to stop.

He started towards her but she held up a hand.

'Just go, Joe.'

'Rachael—' He took another step forward.

'She told you to go.'

Both of them whirled around to see Declan standing outside the bathroom, wrapped in a hotel robe. Rachael gasped, unable to believe she'd forgotten he was around. She hadn't heard the shower stop, neither had she heard him come out. How long had he been there? How much had he heard?

'Declan, I—' Joe began.

Declan walked to his mother's side and put a protective arm about her shoulders. 'Leave us alone.'

Joe took in the determined look on his son's face and realised the boy was serious.

He nodded and without a word, without looking back, he left.

CHAPTER TEN

A WEEK later, Joe was still avoiding Rachael. She'd hardly seen him, just as Helen had initially promised. He was in the clinic for a few hours almost every day but the rest of his time was taken up on set.

Wong had regained consciousness after five days in a coma and was progressing slowly but steadily. Rino was already back on the set, taking over from Wong and making sure the studio lost as little money as possible because of the delays they'd already encountered.

Rachael had spoken to Ethel almost every day and even visited Alwyn once he'd been discharged, and she was glad a lasting friendship seemed to be developing between them. She needed to make new friends.

She'd spoken to Declan about what he'd overheard and after a few days he'd agreed to see Joe. They'd played golf on the weekend and he'd visited the movie set a few more times. Declan seemed to be adjusting to his new life, not only with school but with his father as well.

They moved out of the hotel into their new apartment and finally Rachael started to feel as though she had some sort of control over her life. She had two and a half weeks to go at Joe's practice and then she would need to find somewhere else to work, but the thought of leaving his practice, when she was just starting to get to know her patients, concerned her. She liked it there. Joe wasn't around much, and as the movie still wasn't finished his time at the practice would be minimal. Surely it wouldn't hurt to stay on for her original contract of six months? Declan was getting into a good routine

tine, seeing Joe three times a week after school, and they were planning to play another round of golf this coming weekend.

Rachael resolved to speak to Helen by the end of the day to see if she'd been successful in finding another locum. When she went out to the waiting room, little Anthony Edmunds came running up to her with a book he'd brought from home.

'Read it. Now.' He tugged her to the closest chair and a moment later he'd scrambled up onto her knee and had the book open. Rachael laughed and happily obliged, glad to see Anthony so happy and relaxed. She read it through twice before he'd let her lead him to her consulting room.

'How's everything been this past week?' She flicked through the casenotes, reading the results of the tests.

'He's better and his tantrums have actually decreased,' his mother said.

'That's a positive. The tests show he does have very early diverticulitis but with a healthy diet and regular monitoring, we should be able to treat him without surgical intervention.'

'Oh. You have no idea what a relief that is. I've been trying so hard to get extra fibre into him and yesterday he actually ate what I put in front of him.'

'Good. I'm glad you're being persistent. Keep it up and at the end of next week start introducing a new food. Decrease the amount of liquid paraffin by five mils for the next five days and then decrease by two mils again for seven days. I'll need to review him again then.'

'That's it?'

'Just keep up with those new foods and be persistent. As you've seen, there's been a change in Anthony's attitude and the number of tantrums he's having. His tummy pains are decreasing and that's making him a happier boy.'

His mother smiled. 'You're right.'

'It's a long road.'

'But I'm willing to walk it.'

'That's what I'd hoped to hear.' Rachael took another look

at the X-rays and pointed out the area in question to Anthony's mother.

'It all looks like grey and white swirls to me.'

Rachael smiled as she removed the films. 'Keep doing what you're doing and soon you'll find his dietary fibre levels will be excellent.'

She wrote up the notes after Anthony and his mother had left, and headed back out for her next patient.

'Wendy,' she said, delighted to see the expectant mother again. 'How are you feeling today?'

'Horrible. I have so much back pain it hurts to walk. Is there anything you can give me for it?' Wendy waddled down the corridor.

'When did it start?'

'A few hours ago. No contractions or anything just really bad back pain.'

'OK.' Rachael shut her consulting room door. 'Why don' you get up on the examination bed and we'll check what': going on?' She walked over to the sink, washed her hand: and pulled on a pair of gloves. When Wendy was ready Rachael began the examination, her eyes widening in surprise

A moment later Wendy groaned and closed her eyes. 'Th pain is so bad. It's unbearable. I feel sick.'

'That's because you're in labour.'

'What?' Wendy opened her eyes in total disbelief.

'You're fully dilated.'

'That's impossible. I haven't had any contractions, ju: back pain.'

'Back pain. Contractions.' Rachael shrugged. 'Same diffe ence. Stay where you are.' With her elbow, Rachael presse the intercom button on her phone. 'Helen, Wendy Gibson in labour. The baby is coming…' Wendy groaned in pa again and as she did so, the examination bed and surroundir area became wet as her waters broke. '*Now*. Is Joe in?'

'Yes.'

'I'm going to need him and you. Contact the hospital, the ambulance and Wendy's husband.'

'Rachael!' Wendy called, and Rachael rushed to her side.

'I'm here.' She checked again and wasn't surprised this time to see the baby's head crowning. 'Well, you said your other two children were late. This one is simply impatient.'

'Great. Just what I need,' Wendy groaned.

There was a knock at her door and in the next instant Joe was standing there, his face white with shock. 'Helen told me to get in here.'

'Yes. Get the foetal heart monitor on so we can check the heartbeat. Do Wendy's obs and get ready to take over neonate care once the baby's born. You're doing fine, Wendy.'

'I want to push.'

'Then push.' Rachael continued to assist, conscious of Helen coming in and getting everything organised. Joe had the foetal heart monitor on and the beats coming through were strong and steady, no sign of distress.

'How are you feeling, Wendy?' Rachael asked as the contraction eased. 'Still feel sick?'

'Yes.'

'Bucket's at the ready,' Helen soothed, pushing the hair out of the woman's eyes. 'Your hubby's on his way but I think baby might just beat him here.'

'BP's up but nothing out of the ordinary,' Joe reported. He moved around the room, opening cupboards and getting things ready.

'Ow, ow. The pain's coming again.' Wendy shook her head. 'I'm not ready. The baby can come next week. Any time after this weekend, but not now. Aargh.' She pushed again and the head came out just a little bit more.

'You know how kids are,' Rachael soothed. 'They never listen to their parents.'

'Well, why did this one have to start so early?' Wendy complained. 'It's not fair.'

'I know.' Rachael laughed. 'My son was exactly the same except he thought a midnight delivery was more exciting.'

Joe put the monitor on Wendy's stomach again and met Rachael's gaze as they counted the beats together. 'Good.'

Wendy pushed once more and the head was almost out. 'You're doing a brilliant job. Snatch a breath and push again. Squeeze Helen's hand if you want. Turn it purple. Helen won't mind.' Rachael smiled at the other woman.

'Not at all.' Helen put a wet facecloth on Wendy's brow to cool her down. 'I've plenty of experience assisting with births so trouble me for anything you want.'

'I want my husband,' Wendy growled, before relaxing.

'He's coming. He'll be here soon,' Helen promised.

'Two more pushes and the head will be out. You can do it.' She wiped the area and got ready as Wendy began to push again. 'That's it. That's it. Keep it coming.'

Wendy growled, yelled and let her temper show. Joe checked the baby's heartbeat, glad to find it still strong and steady.

'Where is everyone?' came a loud call.

'In here.' Joe headed to the corridor and soon Wendy's husband was by her side, taking over the hand-holding from Helen.

'This is it, Wendy. One big push and the head will be out.' As the contraction hit, Wendy pushed. Rachael found herself holding her breath in sympathy, her teeth clenched as she mentally pushed with her patient. 'That's it. Snatch a breath. Keep going.' She felt Joe come to stand behind her as the head finally came out. 'That's it. Head's out. Now, don't push. I'm just checking the neck while the shoulders rotate.' She ran her fingers around the baby's neck and, sure enough, there was the cord. 'Joe.' She worked to unloop the cord as Joe held the baby's head. 'Don't push, Wendy.'

'I have to. I need to.' Before she'd finished speaking, the contraction came. Rachael frantically pulled the cord free first one shoulder came out, then the other, and in the next instant the latest edition to the Gibson family entered the world. With one loud gurgling breath, the most beautiful sound in all the world pierced the air around them…the cry of a newborn babe.

Joe held the baby while Rachael found the clamps Helen had laid out and set about getting the cord ready for the baby's dad to cut.

'So what do we have?' Wendy asked impatiently.

Joe held the baby up.

'We have a girl?' Wendy couldn't believe it. Tears overflowed as she gazed with love on her child. Her husband kissed her warmly. Rachael felt the emotions rise within herself and glanced at Joe. He was watching her, and as their gazes held, the feelings between them were raw and real. She saw the love he felt for her in his eyes and she wrapped herself up in that knowledge.

'Ready for the cord?' Helen asked, purposely breaking the fog surrounding Joe and Rachael.

'Uh…yes.' Rachael brought her attention back to the task at hand and soon the new father had cut the cord and Joe took the baby over to Rachael's desk where she realised he'd prepared an area and draped it with soft towels so he could use the small, portable suction machine to clear the baby's mouth and nose. The little girl yelled at him and Rachael laughed.

'You're losing your touch, Joe.'

'Keep quiet,' he grumbled good-naturedly, not bothering to look at her. He couldn't. The one glance they'd just shared had left him naked. Throughout the delivery, he'd been completely aware of Rachael and how she would have gone through this experience without him. He hadn't been there. Wendy's whole attitude had changed when her husband had arrived, and Joe realised just how much he'd really missed of Declan's life. Right now, he would give anything to go back and be able to see his son being born.

'I think I'm getting old,' he said softly to his charge. All she did was wave her arms and legs in the air and cry. 'One-minute Apgar—eight.'

'Excellent.' Rachael and Helen were concentrating on the third stage of labour.

'I've made such a mess,' Wendy said apologetically.

'As if we care about that,' Helen remarked.

Rachael glanced over to where Joe was and couldn't help the way her mouth dropped open to see him carefully wrapping and then cradling the small infant in his arms. It looked so right, so perfect to see him holding the child. How could he possibly think he wouldn't make a great father? She loved him so much and she desperately wanted to show him all he was capable of giving, if only he'd let go and trust her once more.

He looked across at her and they shared another moment before a slow smile spread across his face as he handed the baby to her proud mother.

'Congratulations.'

'Thank you, Dr Silvermark. Oh, she's so perfect.'

'Yes, she is.' Joe was looking at Rachael as he spoke. She was brilliant. She hadn't panicked, she'd done her job, and now there was a healthy baby to show for it. So much could have gone wrong but it hadn't, and the ambulance sirens could be heard in the distance, ready to take the family off to hospital.

Joe quickly cleaned up, setting Rachael's desk back to rights, while he listened to Helen taking charge of the situation.

'I'll ring Patty and she can pick your boys up from school and bring them to the hospital.'

'Thank you,' Wendy replied. 'And to you, Rachael. You were wonderful.'

Rachael smiled and leaned over to brush her finger over

the little girl's forehead. 'She's beautiful. Do you have a name?'

'Cynthia.' Wendy kissed her baby. 'Nick and Elliot are going to be so happy they have a sister. They didn't want a brother.'

'Just as well. Welcome to the world, Cynthia.'

Rachael couldn't take her eyes off the beautiful baby who, after her impatience to be born, had now settled down to sleep. Joe watched Rachael watching the baby and felt the old inadequacies surface once more. She'd mentioned she wanted more children and the thought of her having them with anyone but him made him crazy. Declan didn't deserve half-brothers and sisters but siblings who shared the same parents… But he'd vowed *never* to have children. He'd never wanted to risk hurting them as he'd been hurt by his parents.

The sirens had stopped and as both Helen and Rachael were busy, Joe headed out to let the paramedics in. It was his chance to escape, knowing Rachael was more than capable of taking care of things.

He needed to think.

'Where's Joe?' Declan asked when he arrived at the clinic after school.

'Not sure,' Rachael replied. One of her patients had called to cancel at the last minute so it looked as though she could finish early for once. 'Check with Helen.'

Declan disappeared and came back a moment later with a photograph. 'Hey, Mum. Get a load of this.' He held out a photograph. Rachael looked, then frowned.

'I don't remember this being taken. Where was it? You look about eleven.'

'It's not me, it's Joe.'

'Wow!' Rachael took the photo from him and peered at it more closely. 'That's amazing. I couldn't tell the difference.'

'Helen brought it in for me. She said I could keep it.'

'That's very nice of her.'

'She's a nice lady. I like her.'

Rachael smiled. 'I'm glad to hear it.'

'Mum, are you really going to leave here at the end of the month?'

'Funny you should ask that.' She told him her thoughts about staying on and he dragged her out to the front desk so she could discuss it with Helen.

'Of course you can stay, but are you sure you want it just for your locum contract? You don't want to go down the partnership track?'

'I don't want Joe to feel pressured.'

'Rachael, I'm going to stick my nose in again. How do you feel about Joe?' Helen watched her closely.

'She loves him,' Declan answered for her.

Rachael nodded. 'I always have. Joe's it as far as I'm concerned.'

'And he knows this?'

'Yes.'

'Ah. No wonder he's retreated to his cave.'

'Yes.'

'Cave?' Declan frowned at the two women. 'What cave? Why didn't he take me? I'd like to go caving.'

'Not that sort of cave, darling.' Rachael laughed.

'Give him the time he needs,' Helen advised.

'How long's that?'

Helen shrugged. 'Your guess is as good as mine.'

'Things seemed OK during the delivery. He kept smiling at me.'

'I saw.'

'Delivery?' Declan frowned. 'I don't know what you two are on about but if Joe's not here, I guess we're not going to practise our golf swings, so can we go home, Mum?'

Rachael felt Declan's disappointment. 'Sure. Go get you schoolbag.'

'He's new to this father stuff,' Helen defended Joe. 'And his head's all wrapped up in emotions. And, believe me, emotions aren't Joe's strong point.'

'Tell me about it.' Rachael looked at her watch and then back to Helen. 'Want to come over to our new apartment for dinner?'

Helen beamed. 'Are you kidding? That would be wonderful and I'm dying to see the place.'

'Excellent.'

Joe sat on the beach for hours, just watching life go by. His life had gone by pretty quickly and suddenly he'd found himself getting closer to forty. What had Rach said? The older you get, the better you know yourself. She was right. He knew himself better now than he had at nineteen.

He knew he loved her and it was a love that had never died but had lain dormant for years until she'd walked back into his life. He loved the strong, independent woman she'd become—admired her courage. He knew she would go on living her life without him if that was what he wanted but, he finally admitted to himself, it *wasn't* what he wanted.

You're not into happy families.

Declan's words, combined with the pain he'd witnessed in his son's eyes, filtered through his mind. Happy families was what Rachael and Declan wanted…no, needed, and amazingly he realised he needed it, too.

He knew she loved him, she'd told him so and he'd seen it in her eyes when they'd delivered little Cynthia. But what about the future? Did she really want to build one with him? He frowned as another thought came to mind. Knowing there was only one way to get the answer, he stood up, carelessly brushed the sand away and headed to his car.

Five minutes later, he was knocking on Rachael's apartment door. He was surprised when Helen opened it.

'Aha. Didn't expect to see me here, did you? We've just

finished dinner. Declan's on the phone with a friend and Rachael's in the kitchen.'

'No, she's not. She's here,' Rachael said from behind Helen as she wiped her hands on a dish towel. 'You OK?'

'Yeah. I wanted to apologise to Declan for not being there this afternoon.'

'He won't be long. Come on in,' she instructed, as they were all standing in the doorway. 'You want the guided tour?'

Joe smiled and shoved his hands deep into his jeans pocket. 'Sure.'

'I'll finish up in the kitchen,' Helen said, and tactfully disappeared.

'Well, this is the living area and over here…' Rachael walked to an archway '…is the hallway, and we have Declan's bedroom down there and mine at the other end.'

'Mmm-hmm.' He followed behind, watching the gentle sway of her hips as she spoke. She'd changed from the clothes she usually wore to work into a denim skirt which came to mid-thigh, revealing her sublime legs. Her T-shirt was big and baggy and looked comfortable. Her hair was loose, her face devoid of make-up and she was barefoot, with painted toenails and a toe ring. He raised his eyebrows and when she realised he was looking down at her feet, she smiled.

'A present from Declan. To keep me young at heart.'

'No piercings? Tattoos?'

'No.'

'Glad to hear it.' He leaned back against the wall in the small hallway. She leant against the opposite wall, facing him.

'Are you here to look at the apartment or me?'

'You.' He took her left hand in his and after a moment gently slid the simple wedding band off her finger. 'Hope you don't mind,' he said. Rachael gasped as her insides churned with longing…but she didn't try to stop him.

He looked at the ring closely, reading the inscription '"Rach, love Joe".' He nodded slowly. 'Do you wear th

because it was the only wedding band you could find to protect yourself from scrutiny, or do you wear it because you
couldn't bear to take it off?'

'How important is my answer? I mean, will it alter things?'

'Are you going to be stubborn about this?'

'Are you going to answer my question?'

'Yes, it's important and, no, it won't alter things. I just want
to know.'

Her heart was pounding wildly against her chest. 'You put
it there, Joe, and I couldn't bring myself to take it off. Call
me corny, sappy or whatever else you want, but—'

Her words were cut short as he moved like lightning and
pressed his mouth to hers. His body heat warmed her through
and through as they hungrily took from each other.

'It's been way too long since you kissed me,' she panted
as they broke apart briefly to snatch a breath. He pressed her
back against the wall, covering her body with his, needing to
get as close as possible to the woman of his dreams.

'Rachael. Rachael,' he panted after a few moments. He
pressed kisses around her face, on her neck, before heading
home to her mouth again where he forced himself to slow
down. The sweet and subtle seduction in his kiss only made
her melt even more and finally, when he broke free and gently
caressed her cheek with the back of his fingers, he said, 'You
were the last person I ever wanted to see again…and you
were the only person I ever wanted to see again.'

'I know what you mean. Joe?' She kissed his fingers as
they trailed across her lips. 'Can you tell me? About the past?'

'Yes.' He walked back into the living room and shut the
door. 'It's time. Have a seat.'

Rachael did as she was asked and waited. He paced the
room, glanced unseeingly at pictures on the walls and finally
stopped just before her.

'I had no one, Rach. I look at you and the way you are
with Declan and I envy that. I had no one until Helen found

me, but that's jumping too far ahead.' He took a deep breath. 'I'd learned at an early age not to show my true emotions. From my earliest memory, I was shoved aside if I cried. I was about four years old and my father was yelling at me for something—I can't remember what—and I started to cry and he gave me a backhand right across the face. It was so hard it knocked me off the chair. Then he walked away.'

Rachael watched the controlled emotions as he spoke. She could feel his pain and anguish and her own heart cried out for that little boy who'd been abused.

'It didn't get better. Time and time again he'd hit me. Then he started hitting me just for the fun of it. If I cried, he just hit me harder so I learned not to.' There was an edge to his voice, one she hadn't often heard. 'I'm not telling you this to shock you and I certainly don't want your pity. I want you to know why I pushed you away.'

'I got too close.'

'Yes.'

'All you told me was that you'd been in foster homes and that finally you were old enough to earn some money and escape to travel the world.'

'There's a lot more to it than that.'

'So I figured at the time, but I didn't want to push. When we first met, you were funny and crazy and the most exciting person I'd ever met. You were also one of the smartest.' She smiled. 'Remember how we stayed up late while travelling on the bus, just talking?'

Joe smiled at her. 'From politics to music.'

'We didn't always agree…'

'But, then, who does?' He sat beside her and cupped her face in his hands. 'You were amazing. So caring and accepting. No one had ever treated me like that before. Not in such a personal and romantic way.' He brushed his lips tenderly over hers, drawing those emotions deep into his soul. He looked down into her eyes, still amazed to find her love him had never died. He could see it reflected in every part of her and it made him feel…special.

Joe knew he had to continue the sordid recount of his past, astonished to find how easy it was to say these things to her. He should have known. This was *Rachael*. The woman who loved him. He brushed one last kiss across her lips before moving away.

Again she waited patiently for him to continue.

'I'd always been put down, even in the foster homes which weren't much better than my real home.'

'Did you live on the streets?'

'Yes. Believe it or not, it was safer.' He shrugged. 'At least in a gang I had people looking out for me. We were all in the same boat, beaten by our parents or foster-parents, and had no one to care for us.'

'So you *cared*—in a very broad sense of the word—for each other.'

'Yes. Getting away from everything, from the streets, from the violence that surrounded me, getting away was all I could think about. It was what kept me going. It was what kept me sane. I dropped out of school and got a job in a junkyard. It was easy money and mindless work. I was still in the gang and although I had several brushes with the law, I was thankfully never convicted.'

'What with?'

'Stealing cars. Sometimes stealing food. At one of the foster places I was in, they wouldn't feed us so we'd sneak down to the kitchen at night and raid the place.'

'Why wouldn't they feed you?'

'The government gave them money to be foster-parents and they just took it all and left us with nothing. They'd put a lock on the food cupboard but I learned how to pick locks at a very young age.'

'What happened?' Rachael was astounded.

'You mean when they found the food gone? I'd get beaten because I was the oldest.'

'You stuck up for the others.'

'They were just kids.'

'And you were? What? Thirteen?'

'Yes.' Joe looked out the dark window, his back rigid. 'One night we ate all the food—even the onions—we were so hungry. I was beaten so badly I ended up in hospital. That's when Helen stepped in.'

'She cared about you.'

Joe turned and looked over his shoulder at Rachael. 'Yes. Took me years to trust her but she saved me from being made a ward of the State and put into a shelter. That's when I started to let myself open up a bit.'

'Did she foster you?'

'Not officially. In those days, you had to be married. She did what she could, though. When I was sixteen, she fixed up a small shack for us to live in, made sure we had food.'

'Who's we?'

'My brother—John.' Joe looked back out the window. 'He was a wild one but I managed to keep him out of the courts. I felt responsible for him.'

'What about Melina? Do you have other…siblings?'

'I had three half-brothers and two half-sisters. Two of my brothers died when they were toddlers.'

'Oh, Joe!' Tears sprang instantly to her eyes and she stood desperate to go to him. He didn't turn around and she placed her hands on his shoulders, massaging gently.

'Melina's the only one I keep in contact with. I don't know where the others are.'

'And John?'

Joe shook his head and turned, dragging her into his arms. He rested her head on his chest, content to hold her for moment. 'As I said, I worked for years, slowly getting better jobs until I had enough money to go overseas and lose mysel

That trip to America was my freedom trip. It was proof to myself that I could do what I wanted, that I didn't have to follow rules set by anyone else. I could make my own life. My own rules. I planned to do a quick tour, then find somewhere I liked and settle down to work. Didn't know where or what but I was going to be free.' Joe raked his hand through his hair and pulled back to look at her. 'And then I met you.'

'And then you met me.'

'You were so different from the other girls I'd…dated.'

'Meaning I came from a family with money?'

He grimaced but didn't deny it. 'There was that, but that wasn't why I was attracted to you, Rach. In fact, your wealthy background was a turn-off, but for those three weeks we were together, I pushed away the outside world. There was no rich or poor, no right or wrong—just you and me.'

'And then I got too close.'

'You drive me insane, Rachael. My need for you drives me insane, and it scares me that I can't control myself.'

She bit her lip. 'I'm sorry, Joe. I don't mean to get too close.'

'I know. You've got closer than any other woman, and back then I was astounded at how astute you were. I can't believe I actually married you but I couldn't help myself. I wanted you so badly.'

'But as you've said, you could have just talked me into your bed. So why suggest we go down the "Las Vegas impulsive marriage" track?'

He grinned. 'Because it seemed like fun. And…' He paused and met her gaze. The smile disappeared from his face as he became serious once more. 'And because I felt you deserved better than to be just a roll in the hay.'

'Deserved better? Hmm. So you married me and then broke my heart.' She nodded. 'I think I would have preferred the hay. At least I wouldn't have built a world on false promises.'

'I deserved that.'

'Yes.'

Joe hung his head and exhaled harshly. It was time to face the past, to tell her the truth, and although he'd taught himself from a very early age to remain numb when anything personal came his way, he knew what he was going to say would hurt her.

'So why *did* you marry me?' She pulled back to really look at him.

'It's simple.' His gaze didn't waver as he spoke. 'I married you…because I loved you. Acknowledging that scared the life out of me but the thought of you with any other guy…' Joe clenched his hands into fists and shook his head. 'I couldn't stomach it.'

'So why end it? If you loved me, if you wanted me with you…*why*? Help me to understand, Joe, because I don't. I never have. One minute we were happy and the next—*bam!* You were ripping my heart into tiny little pieces and discarding them.'

'You're right. You deserve to know.' He closed his eyes his voice carefully controlled. 'You remember that second morning? Of course you do,' he muttered, answering his own question. 'On that second morning I got a phone call from Helen.'

'Helen?'

'Yes.' He opened his eyes. 'She'd been trying for days to track me down through the tour organisers and finally succeeded.' He paused, his gaze darkening as he remembered. 'You were in the shower.'

It was all coming back to her now, as though it had happened only yesterday. She'd left their bed and had gone to shower, waiting for Joe to join her as he had every other time she'd left his side. That time he hadn't. She'd told herself not to be concerned that he hadn't come into the shower, yet when she'd returned to the bedroom, he'd already got dressed and had been sitting on the edge of the bed with his head in his hands.

'I asked you what was wrong.'

Joe cleared his throat and tried to get his thoughts back in gear. His mind had mentally stalled at the memory of Rachael in the shower, while his body just ached even more to have her with him beneath the spray once more. 'Yes.' He focused. 'You asked what was wrong and I…I turned my pain and my anger on you. I told you I didn't want to be married any more and that I'd only done it as a joke.'

Rachael's throat choked up at hearing those awful words again. 'I'm glad you remember it word for word.'

'Rachael.' Joe placed his hands on her shoulders, his touch almost begging her to understand. 'I'm *so* sorry.' His words were heartfelt and imploring. She could see the pain and anguish in his eyes and knew he finally spoke the truth about that fateful day. 'I knew I'd hurt you, but I had to.'

'Why?'

'Because John had been arrested for armed robbery and had hung himself in gaol.'

'What?' Rachael couldn't believe it. 'Joe. Joe.' She gathered him to her and wrapped her arms about his waist. 'Why didn't you just tell me? I could have been there for you. I helped you. I was your wife!'

Joe hesitated. 'I couldn't tell you *because* you were my wife.'

'What?' She stared up at him. 'That doesn't make any sense.'

'When Helen called and told me about John, it was like a slap in the face. The real world had intruded into our private space of heaven, and I knew I couldn't drag you back into my real world. It was different from yours and I could never hope to give you the things you needed.'

'All I needed was you, Joe.'

'No. Rachael, we were young and I had no idea what I

wanted to do with my life. You'd already been accepted to medical school and had a life planned—a life I would never have fitted into. I felt so worthless…and I knew with such clarity that in time—if we'd stayed together—you would come to realise I *was* worthless.'

'Joe.' She was appalled. 'How could you think that?'

'We were from different worlds. It didn't matter what I *wanted*, it would never happen. John was my brother—my *real* brother. Same mother, same father, and together we'd seen it all. Street fights, gangs, murders, and all by the time I was twelve. We'd been beaten, abused and shoved from one foster family to the next. I did things I'm not proud of and the memories will plague me for the rest of my life, regardless of how sorry I am for ever doing them. I hurt other people because it was the only way I knew to cope.'

Rachael didn't want to hear it but at the same time knew she needed to. She needed to be part of his pain, part of his past if anything was going to happen between them in the future.

'It brought everything home, Rachael. It made me realise I had to push you away. Right then, right there.'

'But we could have worked through things.'

'You would have been hurt worse if we'd tried to make a go of it.'

'I doubt that.'

'It would have been worse.'

'How can you say that?' she pushed.

'Because I know!' Joe ground out, and let her go so he could pace once more. 'Think about it, Rach. What would I have done when we returned to Australia? Where would we have lived? With your parents? In a nice, cushy town house they would have bought you? No. I'm a man who needs to be in control and I wouldn't have been in that situation. Besides, you had six years of medical school ahead of you and the only plan I had was to avoid Australia and become a professional beach bum.'

'And did you?'

Joe exhaled and shook his head. 'I tried to, but four months after John's death my best friend was attacked by a shark. We were surfing at night in Hawaii, and everything happened so fast. I managed to get him back to shore but he died soon after. I didn't know what to do. I didn't know how to save him. If I'd even known CPR, I could have done something. It was then I realised that if I'd been more like you, more dedicated to finding a path for my future, had done a first-aid course, I might have been able to save him or at least get him breathing again until help arrived.'

Her heart went out to him even more and she wanted to comfort the lost boy she saw before her. The number plate on his car now made perfect sense. So many things *had* happened when he was nineteen…life-changing things.

'You can't blame yourself for his death. Depending on how bad he was, he probably would have been in shock and it would have taken a medical professional to be there on the spot to save him.' Rachael paused. 'It wasn't your fault and neither was John's death.'

'It's taken me years to work through that, but you're right. Regardless, after the shark incident, I sat down and did some hard thinking. That's when I decided what to do with my life.'

'To become a doctor?'

'Yes. You'd given me the idea and the surfing trauma and John's senseless death cemented it.'

'I gave you the idea? Joe, I never once suggested you needed to change.'

'No, you didn't. You accepted me for me, just as you've done now. You've put your heart on the line once more, which shows just how much you trust me.'

'Love is nothing without trust, Joe.'

'You're right. You're so right.' Telling her about his past, about John, had lifted an enormous weight from his shoulders.

'Thank you, Joe. Thank you for opening up to me.' She touched the hair at his temple. 'I know how hard it was for you.'

'It was long overdue.'

'Still…thank you.' She wanted him to know she understood the enormity of what he'd revealed. 'But there's just one more thing I need to know.' She held her breath for a second before asking, 'Do you love me? Can you say it' Because I can see it, I can feel it, but I need the words, Joe.

'I know, sweetheart.' He edged back and looked at her, hi blue eyes gazing down into hers. 'I love you, Rachael. I al ways have and I always will.' He confirmed his words wit a bone-melting kiss. When her knees gave way, he held he closer.

'I'm part of a package deal, Joe.'

'I know, and you already know how much I love Decla but I'm going to need help with the parenting thing.'

She smiled. 'My advice to you…just be yourself, Joe. know how tough that is for you, to open up to someone, b don't shut him out or you'll risk him shutting you out.'

He nodded. 'What about the others?'

'Others?' She frowned and then her eyes widened as h words penetrated the fog beginning to cloud her mind. 'Y want to have more children?'

'Only with you. The thought of you with anyone el churns me up. I want to take care of you, to protect you, help you, to—'

'Smother me?' She laughed. 'Joe, we're a family. We wo together to care, protect and help each other.'

'Rach, what I'm trying to say is I need you. I need you need Declan. I can't go on any more without knowing bo of you are going to be there. You were right when you s:

love creates emotion. It does, and I've been fighting them all my life. I want to stop fighting and start enjoying.'

He took her wedding band from his pocket, and until that moment she'd forgotten he'd taken it off her finger. Then he got down on one knee.

'Joe? What are you doing?' She shook her head but was unable to remove the enormous smile on her face.

'I'm proposing.'

The door to the living room burst open as he spoke.

'You're proposing?' Declan said in a loud voice. Helen came rushing in.

'Did someone mention proposing?'

'Will you both keep quiet and let me do it?' Joe growled.

'Here? In the living room?' Rachael grinned. 'You old romantic, you.'

'Why not? At least it's better than the first time.'

'Where was the first time?' Declan wasn't going anywhere and neither, it seemed, was Helen.

'On a bus with rowdy people all around us. He made a big scene.'

'You loved it.'

She smiled. 'I did. At least we're not being jostled by the bus this time.'

'Are you going to keep quiet?'

'Yes, but only for a second so be quick. I'm already getting excited.'

'Does that mean you'll say yes?'

'Ask the question and find out.'

Joe sobered and took her left hand in his once more. 'Rachael Elizabeth Cusack…' His gaze was intense on hers. There was no one, nothing else—just the two of them. 'I love you, but first I want to ask your forgiveness. I hurt you badly and I never want to do that again. This time it'll be different, I promise. You are my soul mate and I was a fool to let you go. I'm not making the same mistakes again. I'm done running. I want you, I *need* you with me…for ever. Without you, I'm only half a person. Marry me, Rach—make me whole again. Please?'

Rachael closed her eyes for a second, letting go of the pain hurt and humiliation she'd felt in the past. He'd asked her to forgive him, and she did. They would start their new life together with a clean slate.

She took a breath and looked down at him, her heart reflected in her eyes. 'I love you, Joe, so much it hurts when I'm not with you. Of course I'll marry you.'

Declan and Helen whooped for joy but Rachael and Joe continued to ignore them. Joe slowly placed her wedding ring back on her finger before standing to gather her close. He pressed his mouth to hers and felt the same sense of freedom he'd felt when she'd said yes all those years ago.

'Now, where do you want to get married this time, Dr Cusack?'

'Las Vegas.'

'Again? Are you sure?'

Rachael nodded. 'Declan will love it.'

Joe raised his eyebrows wolfishly. 'He's not the only one.' And bent his head to capture her lips in a kiss which would bind them together, as a family, for ever.

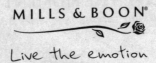

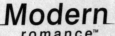 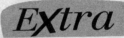

4 FREE

BOOKS AND A SURPRISE GIFT!

We would like to take this opportunity to thank you for reading this Mills & Boon® book by offering you the chance to take FOUR more specially selected titles from the Medical Romance™ series absolutely FREE! We're also making this offer to introduce you to the benefits of the Reader Service™—

- ★ **FREE home delivery**
- ★ **FREE gifts and competitions**
- ★ **FREE monthly Newsletter**
- ★ **Exclusive Reader Service offers**
- ★ **Books available before they're in the shops**

Accepting these FREE books and gift places you under no obligation to buy, you may cancel at any time, even after receiving your free shipment. Simply complete your details below and return the entire page to the address below. You don't even need a stamp!

YES! Please send me 4 free Medical Romance books and a surprise gift. I understand that unless you hear from me, I will receive superb new titles every month for just £2.75 each, postage and packing free. I am under no obligation to purchase any books and may cancel my subscription at any time. The free books and gift will be mine to keep in any case.

M5ZEI

Ms/Mrs/Miss/Mr ....Initials ....
BLOCK CAPITALS PLEASE

Surname ....

Address ....

....

....Postcode..........................

Send this whole page to:
UK: FREEPOST CN8I, Croydon, CR9 3WZ